"I'M GOING TO MAKE YOU WISH YOU'D NEVER BEEN BORN."

The mother vampire threw back her head.

"Vengeance," she shouted, her voice harsh, distorted. "Powers of the Underworld, Powers of Darkness, hear my call. Hear the cry of a mother, begging for retribution. Answer my plea! Give me justice! Rise up and avenge the deaths of my sons!"

Above their heads, as if in answer, from a clear night sky, rolled one clap of thunder.

"I really hate it when they call for reinforcements," Angel said.

"I say we finish this now, before anything else shows up," Buffy said. She took a gliding step forward.

The mother vamp lowered her head and looked straight at her.

"Get ready," she said. "Your doom is coming."

Buffy the Vampire Slayer™

Available from ARCHWAY Paperbacks and POCKET PULSE

Buffy the Vampire Slayer adult books

Available from POCKET BOOKS

BUFFY
THE VAMPIRE
SLAYER™

HERE BE MONSTERS

Cameron Dokey

An original novel based on the hit TV series created by Joss Whedon

POCKET PULSE

New York   London   Toronto   Sydney   Singapore

An *Original* Publication of POCKET BOOKS

 POCKET PULSE, published by
Pocket Books, a division of Simon & Schuster Inc.
1230 Avenue of the Americas, New York, NY 10020

ISBN: 0-671-03921-0

First Pocket Pulse printing June 2000

10 9 8 7 6 5 4 3 2 1

POCKET PULSE and colophon are registered trademarks of Simon & Schuster Inc.

Printed in the U.S.A.

For Team Lisa, especially its fearless leader. You are the best, and the whole world should bow down before you.

For Ellen, my number one Slayer-watching pal.

And for Jim, because everything is.

Historian's Note:
This story takes place in the
third season.

CHAPTER 1

It was a dark and starless night.

In the darkness, in the town that sat atop the Hellmouth, a teenage girl was running for her life.

Definitely not the kind of night she'd had in mind.

Her name was Heidi Lindstrom. Which was a laugh she could have done without. Everybody knew what a girl named Heidi was supposed to be. Sweet. Innocent. Self-sacrificing. She'd put a stop to any hope of that right off.

Heidi Lindstrom was tough, and she made sure she looked it. Hair bleached bone-white stood straight up from her dark-rooted scalp. Jeans as tight as snakeskin covered long legs that, at the moment, were desperately trying to keep on keepin' on. A black leather bomber jacket flapped against her back, the silver studs across the shoulders gleaming dully in the streetlights. Thick-soled black boots encased her feet. Perfect for stepping on anyone who got in her way, but far from good for running.

And she'd been running for a very, very long time now.

So long, she could hardly remember a time when she hadn't been running. A time when she'd felt safe. Or if not safe, then at least in control. A time when her legs didn't feel like rubber and her feet like lead. A time when the air didn't burn going in and out of her lungs.

Long enough for her to feel like she was running in a fever dream, desperately forcing her body to keep on moving even though her thundering heart knew that no speed she could reach was ever going to be fast enough. For all the chance she had, she might as well be moving in slow motion.

She swung left, legs pumping as she pounded up the middle of the street right past a pole holding aloft a green street sign that proudly proclaimed, ELM. She wished she had enough breath left to laugh at the joke. 'Cause this was a nightmare, no two ways about it.

But the truth was, all the streets had tree names in this part of Sunnydale. Oak. Birch. Larch. Poplar. Sycamore. The houses were a whole lot bigger than the one she lived in, every single one fronted by a lush green lawn.

What would happen if I suddenly ran up one of those perfectly manicured front walks? she wondered. Pounded desperately on one perfectly painted front door? Would one of the perfect people who lived there come rushing out to help her?

She did manage to laugh then, a strangled sound wrenched, unbidden, straight from her gut.

Dream on.

This part of Sunnydale might look different, but, in

2

one respect at least, it was the same as the part of town that she came from. Nobody was coming to help her. Not now. Not ever. That was part of what made Sunnydale what it was. There was only one thing she could do, and she was already doing it.

Run. Run. *Run.*

She veered left onto Oak, traveling down the sidewalk now. Trying not to feel the way her legs had turned loose as rubber bands. The way the breath seared like a hot poker thrust into her lungs.

How close are they? Are they gaining? Heidi risked a quick glance over her shoulder, hoping against hope that maybe the miracle had happened and she'd just been too worn out to notice. Maybe they'd finally given up the chase. Gotten bored. Or maybe she'd finally managed to outrun them.

Yeah, right. *That* was likely.

They were still back there, just the way she'd known they would be. Two guys. The ones she'd spotted for the first time in the alley behind the Bronze.

Wearing shirts so white they practically glowed in the dark. Khakis with perfect creases exactly down the center of each pant leg. Penny loafers. *Ties.* The way these guys dressed made parochial school uniforms look like Tommy Hilfiger. When she'd first spotted them, Heidi hadn't been able to help herself. She'd burst out laughing.

But that had been before she'd seen their eyes.

Gleaming. Feral. *Yellow.* Their foreheads looked funny, some weird deformation, maybe. And they needed some orthodontic attention. Big time. Heidi didn't know what they were, and she didn't want to know. The only thing she wanted was to get away from them.

It hadn't been until they'd started to chase her that she'd realized she actually wanted two things.

Heidi Lindstrom also wanted to stay alive.

She sprinted across the intersection of Oak and Poplar. She knew it wouldn't be much longer now. How could it be? Now, she couldn't feel her legs at all.

Why the hell didn't they just close in and finish her off?

End the game. Go for the kill. It was what she would have done. But oh no, not these guys. They had to hold back. Be different. Play cat and mouse. It would have seriously pissed her off, if she hadn't been so terrified.

Nobody messed with Heidi Lindstrom. Instead, she messed with them. That was the way things were supposed to go down. But nothing had gone the way it was supposed to, tonight. Tonight she'd made a mistake. One that was going to cost her everything.

Why couldn't I have just stayed home?

She was stumbling now, her lower body refusing to cooperate. Sweat from her forehead crept down to sting her eyes.

Would it really have been so hard, just this once, to have stayed at home?

Home, where the walls were so thin she could hear right through them. Where the air always smelled of last night's burned dinner. Home, the place that had never been where the heart was. A place where every angry, hurtful thing that had ever been said lived on, forever. The last place on earth she'd rather be.

Particularly when her mother turned the TV on.

She was running doubled over now, both arms pressed against her stomach, the memory of the sound of the television roaring in her mind. It was that sound more than anything else that had made her do it. Climb out her bedroom window and head for the Bronze.

The one place she could forget all the things she was, and all the things she wasn't. Where the music was loud enough to drown the sound of her mother's TV programs from her mind. Always the same sound, night after night.

Show after show filled with families who were warm and caring. Ones where the kids and parents had their problems, sure, but nothing that a little love and good communication couldn't solve. Shows where sooner or later, the kids would admit that the parents were right, had always been right. Would always *be* right. They'd confess their sins, their guilt, their love, then be welcomed with open arms and absolved.

Fantasy families, Heidi thought. She gulped air as she swung down Larch, her breath a white-hot needle stitching through her from side to side.

The trouble was, her mom never seemed to get the fact that those families on the television weren't the real thing, just as she never got the fact that even fantasy kids never gave their love away for nothing.

Those fantasy parents had to get their kids' love the old-fashioned way. By earning it. A fact even the writers of lame-o sitcoms seemed to know. But which, in spite of all the hours of dedicated TV watching she put in, had never once penetrated the brain of Heidi's mom.

Her parenting method usually involved pointing out all the ways that Heidi wasn't good enough. And it always involved telling Heidi what a disappointment she was. If Heidi'd had a nickel for every time her mom had said she didn't understand how a daughter of hers could have turned out this way, she could have had a condo on the beach in Malibu by the time she was nine.

She stumbled as she took the curb at Larch and Sycamore. Her own ragged breathing the only sound.

Sycamore was a transition street, not quite as upscale as the streets around it. The streetlights didn't shine as brightly here, assuming that they even worked at all. The houses had big chunks of brown bark in their front yards instead of lawns. Beauty bark, it was actually called.

It wasn't as clean and cool-looking in the hot Southern California summers, but it sure cut down on the water bill, a thing Heidi had heard her mother say ad nauseum. Though Clara Lindstrom didn't care for beauty bark, herself. Which was why, once a year, she had the local garden center deliver a truckload of those nice sparkly white rocks for the Lindstrom front yard.

Heidi straightened up, got her burning eyes to focus on the end of the street, on the one working streetlight and the bus stop just beyond. If she could make it to the bus stop, a brightly lit public place, would the miracle happen? Would the guys behind her back off and leave her alone?

You can make it, she told herself. *Come on. Come on.*

Desperately, she tried for a last burst of speed. She felt her foot wobble, her ankle twist.

Oh, God, she thought. *Oh, please, God, no.*

And then she was falling, as if in slow motion. She had time to see the thing that had brought her down. A piece of beauty bark skittered out from underneath her foot to lie in the gutter. Just one piece, but it had been **enough**.

Time speeded up again to the sound of Heidi's right elbow cracking against the sidewalk, pistol-shot loud. She screamed as blazing pain roared from her elbow to her shoulder. She rolled onto her back, her right arm flopping uselessly out from her body at a funny angle, and then lay still. Desperately sucking air, her vision went from white, to gray, then fuzzy around the edges as Heidi realized she couldn't feel the pain anymore.

Shock, she thought. The only positive spin on the whole situation was that she was left-handed, something the guys behind her didn't know. When they came to get her, she could still throw one last punch. Assuming she'd be able to do anything at all.

How would her mother feel, she wondered, when she realized her only child was gone for good? That Heidi wasn't ever coming home.

Then she heard the sound of hard-soled shoes against the sidewalk. A moment later, two pairs of yellow eyes were bending over her, gleaming down. Even through her dimming vision, Heidi could tell she'd been right the first time, all those blocks ago behind the Bronze.

These guys were the ugliest suckers she'd ever seen in her entire life. Also the most terrifying.

Not that she was going to let them know that, of course. She'd rather die first. Or second.

She sucked in a breath, cleared her suddenly clogged throat, forced her voice to function. Heidi Lindstrom was not going out like a wuss.

"That's some case of hepatitis."

The guy on the right put his hands on his hips, just like Heidi's mother did when she was annoyed about something. Heidi bit down, hard, on her tongue. Nothing about this situation was the least bit funny. So why did she suddenly have this outrageous impulse to laugh out loud?

Shock, she thought again. And saw the eyes above her waver as the tremors started, deep in her stomach. Cold. She was so very cold.

"Well, I declare," the guy said, his tone colored by a Southern accent thick as library paste. "There's no call to be rude, you know. We won the chase, fair and square. It's not our fault that you fell down."

He took his eyes off Heidi long enough to flick them toward the guy standing next to him, as if looking for support. "Is it, Webster?" he went on.

"No, Percy," yellow-eye on the left answered at once.

The yes-man, Heidi thought.

"It definitely is not," he continued, seriously. "Not our fault at all."

Heidi gave up the fight, released a snort of laughter through her nose. They sounded like something out of an almost-forgotten Saturday morning cartoon.

"What's the matter with her, Percy?" Webster asked anxiously, leaning over to get a better look himself, now.

Percy shook his head. "I do not know, Webster," he responded. "I simply do not know. It is a puzzle, to be sure."

"You don't think she has something contagious, do you?" Webster asked, his tone genuinely alarmed. He straightened up abruptly, as if this might get him out of the range of germs.

"Webster," Percy said.

"What?"

"Try not to be any more stupid than you already are."

Webster's bottom lip poked out. "You're not supposed to talk to me like that," he pouted. "Mama doesn't like it. She told you not to."

Heidi wanted to laugh again, but discovered she couldn't do it. Her ability to command her body seemed to be gone. All she could do was stare upward at the two guys above her, their white shirts blocking out the dark night sky.

Now that she had nothing else to do but look them over, Heidi could see that yellow-eye on the left, the one called Webster, wore a navy blue tie. Percy's tie was a dark maroon. Other than that, they seemed identical. Tough Heidi Lindstrom been brought down by twin cartoon preppies from Hell.

Talk about embarrassing.

Percy leaned closer, as if he wanted to confide something to Heidi. "You were the best so far," he told her. "You lasted at least ten blocks longer than I thought you would. That's twice as long as the last one, isn't it, Webster?"

Being reminded about how good the chase had been seemed to take Webster right out of his snit.

"That's right, Percy," he seconded.

Heidi began to feel like she was floating. She wasn't even cold anymore. She couldn't remember why she'd been so afraid. These guys weren't going to hurt her. They'd chased her halfway across town so they could bore her to death.

It didn't even bother her when Percy dropped to one knee beside her. He reached for her head, turning it from side to side.

"She looks absolutely perfect," he commented. "So, so . . ."

Momentarily, Percy seemed at a loss for words. Fortunately for him, Webster chose that moment to have a light bulb above the head experience.

"So . . . *tacky*," he filled in obligingly.

"Tacky!" Percy echoed, delighted. "Tacky, yes. I think that's it."

"Mother will be so pleased," Webster put in. "This is exactly the kind of girl she's always warned us about."

Oh, give me a break, Heidi thought. *Like the two of you have won so many beauty contests.*

As if from a great distance, she heard the sound of the bus, pulling up to the Sycamore Street stop, the hiss and slap of the doors folding open. A moment later she heard them close again, and the bus rumbled off.

She hadn't made it. Wasn't going to make it. Heidi's numbness vanished as fear and pain came roaring back. She was down. But she wasn't out. Not yet. There was still something she had to do. Something important. Heidi swallowed, got her mouth to open.

"Oh, look!" Webster practically squealed in delight. "She wants to say something."

He knelt down too, until his face was level with Percy's. Heidi looked up into two pairs of gleaming yellow eyes, their expressions watchful, expectant.

What are you? she wondered.

Not that it mattered. No matter what they were, there was really only one thing she wanted to tell them.

It was true that, to do it, she'd have to use a word her mother had proclaimed she never wanted to hear in *her* house. A word that good girls never used. Though Heidi'd always figured it couldn't really be all that bad, because the word she had in mind almost always had a friend.

A little word, like "off" or "you."

She pulled in a deep breath. If she was only going to have the strength to say one more thing, she'd better get it right the first time.

"Please," she was appalled to hear herself whisper. That tore it. Now she'd done it. The thing she hated most of all. She'd gone and used the "p" word.

"Please, don't kill me."

Percy gave a high-pitched squeal of laughter. He sounded exactly like a stuck pig.

"Did you hear that, Webster?" he asked, delighted. "You got us all wrong, miss."

Webster nodded. "Dead wrong," he said.

Then he, too, went off into peals of laughter. The two whatever-they-weres leaned on one another, pounding each other on the backs in their unbridled mirth.

Maybe I should make another run for it while they're overcome by their attack of the jollies, Heidi thought. The only problem with that plan being that she'd have to get up first.

"We're not going to kill you, honey," Percy explained when he'd finally recovered. He wiped his streaming eyes with his maroon tie.

"Don't do that," Webster said. "It's disgusting."

"At least, not yet," Percy continued, ignoring his brother. "There's something very important we have to do first."

"Oh, yes, very important," Webster agreed solemnly. "She wants to know what it is, I can just tell. Don't you want to know what it is, sugar?"

Both guys grinned, completely exposing their disgusting teeth. Fangs. Whatever.

"We're going to take you home to Mother," they said in unison.

Percy cocked his head. "Of course, the fact that we can't kill you yet doesn't mean that you'll enjoy the trip."

"Oh, goody. I just love this part," Webster said.

Percy reached down, and grabbed Heidi by her right arm. She screamed again. Pain roared through her, hot and quick as lightning. Then, just like lightning it was over. The world went black.

She awoke to a world of blinding white and discovered she was lying on her stomach. Her cheek was pressed against something cold and smooth and white with her left arm folded under her. The surface looked just like the marble floor Heidi'd seen once on a school field trip to an art museum.

The pain in Heidi's right arm was so great, her whole body vibrated with it. That was the bad news. The good news was that her head was clearer, and that she couldn't see Webster and Percy.

Slowly, carefully, Heidi leveraged herself up onto her left arm. Maybe if she could get to her feet, she could discover where she was and get the hell out of here.

"Oh, good, you're awake, my dear," a voice behind her said.

Heidi started. Her left arm slipped, jarring her right one and making her head crack back down onto the marble floor. She closed her eyes as fresh, hot pain swept through her.

When she opened her eyes again, there was a woman bending over her.

On her head was the biggest-brimmed straw hat Heidi had ever seen. A gauzy pink scarf was tied around the crown, the ends disappearing down over one of the woman's broad shoulders.

The dress she had on was pink, too. Hot pink. With flowers. Heidi couldn't tell what kind they were, but she could tell that they were really, really big. Pinned to the front of the dress was an enormous rhinestone brooch. So enormous Heidi could see herself reflected in the center stone.

This just had to be Big Mama, the woman the twin twerps had brought Heidi home to meet. And those boys had had the nerve to call *her* tacky.

"I'm so happy you could join us, my dear," Big Mama said.

Well, goody for you, Heidi thought. *At least that makes one of us.*

Big Mama's voice had the same accent Webster and Percy's did. Like a *Gone With the Wind* extra. But at least her face looked comparatively normal. Her eyes weren't yellow. And her teeth all seemed to fit inside her mouth when she closed it.

"I hope my boys weren't too hard on you," Big Mama said. "They can be a little impetuous sometimes. Still, boys will be boys, won't they? I'm sure you understand."

What Heidi understood was that Big Mama had definitely flunked Feminism 101. She licked her cracked lips, tried her voice and discovered it worked.

"They broke my arm," she croaked out.

"Did not," a voice contradicted at once, from somewhere over Heidi's right shoulder. Heidi figured it was probably Percy. He almost always spoke up first. Plainly, the twin twerps were there somewhere, skulking in the background.

"She fell down, Mama. We were nowhere near her when it happened, were we, Webster?" the voice went on.

"No, we weren't," Webster seconded his brother. "We caught her fair and square. I promise, Mama."

"Now, now, boys," their mother chided. "You know it's not polite to contradict a guest."

Heidi heard a strange sound coming from behind her. A sound she could have sworn was Percy and Webster shuffling their feet.

"There, there," Big Mama said, her tone soothing. She straightened up. Standing, she looked like a big pink tower. "Mama knows you're her good boys. It doesn't matter how you caught her. What matters is that you brought the food home just the way I asked you to. You know how I worry about what you boys might put in your mouths."

Heidi felt cold sweat break out on her forehead. *Food?* This definitely did not sound good. At all. In fact, it sounded downright—Heidi's mind sheared away. She didn't really want to think too much about what that sounded like. If she did, she was afraid that she'd start screaming and never stop.

"Help the girl up, Webster," said Big Mama. "I want to take a nice long look at her. Oh, no, my dear," she went on, as Heidi desperately tried to scoot away. "It's all right. He won't hurt you. Not until I say so. Nothing in this house happens without my permission."

"Gee, thanks," Heidi gasped. "Suddenly, I just feel so much better."

Big Mama threw back her head and gave a laugh that sounded like fingernails being scraped across a chalkboard.

"Such a spirited young thing," she commented. "But spirits can be broken, you know, my dear. It happens every single day. Actually, I've been known to break a few myself."

Without warning, her face twisted, morphing into an even more hideous version of her sons'. Her forehead folded in upon itself until it was nothing but a series of deep grooves. Her eyes turned wolf-yellow.

"I said *help her up*, Webster. You know how I hate to be kept waiting. It isn't nice to disappoint your Mama."

Heidi felt herself seized and hauled to her feet by a strong grip on her left arm. She swayed, and the grip tightened, keeping her from falling.

"Here she is, Mama."

The second Webster spoke, Big Mama's face relaxed. The skin on her forehead smoothed out. Her eyes resumed their normal, washed-out blue color.

Heidi locked her knees to keep them from knocking together. *I know what you are*, she thought. *You're monsters.*

The kind her mother had promised her didn't exist, though Heidi had always been quite sure they did.

Looks like I was right about one thing, Mama.

And because she was, Heidi knew that there was only one way this could end. The way she'd always known it would.

She was going to die.

She hoped it would be quick. And that she was dead before they did that thing that sounded like Heidi was going to be a midnight snack. Out of all the freaks in Sunnydale, she'd had to come across the ones who were close personal friends of Hannibal Lecter.

Heidi stood perfectly still as Big Mama started to circle like a shark, her high heels clicking against the cold white marble.

"Horrible," Mama murmured, as her eyes took in Heidi's jeans and leather. "Absolutely dreadful. You've chosen well, boys. This one is really only fit for one thing." She stepped up close. Webster released Heidi and backed off. Heidi felt her knees begin to buckle.

"Come with me, my dear," Big Mama said, slipping her arm through Heidi's before she could fall. Heidi winced. Big Mama might look like a marshmallow in a pink flowered tent, but she had a grip like a steel trap.

"I want to show you something."

The toes of Heidi's shoes dragged as Big Mama spun her around and pulled her across the room. Heidi was pleased to note she'd left ugly dark skidmarks on the clean white floor.

"This is my boys' heritage," Big Mama announced, as she gestured toward the wall. On it was a series of paintings. Portraits.

That's why this place reminded me of an art museum, Heidi realized. *Because it's a portrait gallery.*

Each painting was illuminated by two old-fashioned brass lights, one on the top, one on the bottom. They gave the portraits a strange, otherworldly look. As if their eyes really would follow you when you moved around the room. They reminded Heidi of something. What was it?

Stern men in topcoats and glossy black boots stood beside tired-eyed women in long, shawl-draped dresses. Solemn children wore long curls, were dressed in frilly white shirts and lace-up boots so that Heidi couldn't tell the girls from the boys.

"My boys come from a proud heritage, a long line of true ladies and gentlemen," Big Mama went on. "That man over there—" She gestured toward the portrait of a man standing beside a big black horse. "—was one of the founding fathers of the Commonwealth of Virginia. And here—"

She jockeyed Heidi into position in front of the largest portrait in the entire gallery, a man wearing the gray uniform of a Confederate officer.

"Here is my boys' father," Big Mama said, the pride in her voice actually making it sound warm. "Boys," she cooed. "Go over there and stand beside the portrait of your papa."

Webster and Percy complied, moving to stand on either side of their father's portrait. They looked like puppies, eager to please. *Mutant puppies just waiting to eat me.* Heidi felt her stomach roll over.

"My husband was the finest man who ever lived," said Big Mama. "And I've raised my boys to be true gentlemen, just like him. When my husband was tragically cut down in the prime of his life, I knew my duty: to protect my babies. To be with them, always."

Heidi felt Big Mama's gaze upon her. Plainly, the other woman expected her to say something. Heidi pulled in a deep breath and considered her options.

Her right arm was broken. Her left arm in Mama's tight grip. All around her, there were monsters. Heidi knew that she was never going to leave this place alive. But was that the same as being helpless? Did it mean she had to go gentle into that good night? Whatever that meant.

She didn't think so. Particularly since she realized what the paintings all around her reminded her of.

"I'll bet these portraits are like the ones in the Haunted House in Disneyland, aren't they?"

Big Mama's face went completely blank, but she was a lady first, last, and always. And a lady never forgot her manners.

"I beg your pardon?"

Heidi grinned. It felt good to go out with a bang, she thought. Even if it was only a small one.

"You know—they look normal when you first come in, but then they stretch and stretch and you can see they're all disgusting on the bottom. I'll bet these paintings are just like that. Good looking on top, sick underneath."

Heidi cocked her head in the direction of Big Mama's dearly departed spouse. "Especially that one. Your precious boys are like that, too. I knew they were freaks the first moment I saw them."

Big Mama threw back her head and bellowed. Her grip on Heidi's arm tightened so that Heidi saw stars. When her vision cleared again, she knew she was looking into the face of her own death. Straight up into the eyes of the monster.

"You horrible, mannerless, insolent girl," Big Mama hissed through long, sharp teeth as her eyes blazed fierce and yellow. "You are the one who is disgusting. You're only fit to be one thing: Dead meat."

With one vicious yank, she pulled Heidi's head to one side and sank her teeth into the jugular.

Heidi had time for just one thought. *This can't be true. Can't be happening. In horror movies, yes. In real life, no.*

Then she couldn't think at all as her body began to spasm out of control, twitching and jerking like a live wire. Big Mama roared again, lifting her blood-stained face. Then she spun Heidi around and thrust her toward her sons.

"Take her," Heidi heard Big Mama gasp.

And then Webster and Percy were on her.

One on either side they fastened themselves onto her throat. Heidi didn't move at all now. She couldn't. All she could do was stand stock-still, her mouth working helplessly, her eyes staring straight ahead at the portrait of their father, as Webster and Percy drank their fill.

She stayed standing for one final moment after they were through. After they'd lifted their heads and released her. After they'd stepped back, once more, to stand side by side beneath the portrait of their dear, departed father.

Through her dimming vision, Heidi saw Big Mama move to stand between her sons, put her arms around them. They rested their heads on her ample, pink-flowered bosom. Heidi's life's blood stained their mouths. Above their heads, Heidi swore she saw the portrait smiling down upon them.

"My good boys," Heidi heard Big Mama coo. Heidi's legs buckled, then refused to hold her. "You were so tidy. You didn't spill a drop. You make your Mama so proud of you."

Heidi felt herself falling. She saw the marble floor rush up toward her. Her head cracked against it, but by then, it didn't matter. Because by then, it was all over.

By the time her head split open on the cold, white stone, Heidi Lindstrom felt nothing. Saw nothing. Heard nothing.

Was nothing.

And so she never heard the only epitaph that she would ever receive.

"Get that disgusting piece of trash out of here," said Big Mama.

Chapter 2

The animals were hungry, and Buffy Summers had made a big mistake. She'd arrived right at feeding time.

In her job as the Chosen One, the Slayer, Buffy had seen some pretty horrific things in her young life. But this was enough to make even the Slayer's iron-clad stomach turn.

Tongues flicked out. Jaws opened. Saliva dripped. Teeth parted, then bit down. Hard. Gelatinous red stuff gushed and spurted. And there wasn't a damn thing Buffy could do about it. She was completely helpless. Powerless in the face of the most disgusting sight she'd ever been forced to witness.

In the daytime anyway.

It was lunchtime at the food court in the Sunnydale mall.

"Hungry, honey?" Joyce Summers asked as she joined her daughter at the edge of the food court. Buffy watched in sick fascination as the guy at the table closest to her hefted a clump of French fries. He dunked them into a plastic cup containing what had to be at least half a bottle of ketchup, then lifted them up. High.

He tilted his head back, waiting until one pendulous gob of ketchup had dropped down onto his tongue, then stuffed the clump of fries into what Buffy could only think of as his gaping maw. He chewed, ketchup gathering in the corners of his mouth, then wiped his face with the back of his hand and reached for a second handful.

Buffy looked away. Call her a wimp, but she just didn't think she could take any more of this.

"I don't think so, Mom."

Joyce Summers shrugged. "Okay," she said agreeably. "If you say so. But I thought that's why you came over here."

I thought so too, Buffy silently acknowledged, as she watched a French fry hit the table out of the corner of her eye. What was it with guys and food, anyway? she wondered. For something they considered so important, they sure seemed to have more than their fair share of manual dexterity problems about it.

Buffy took her mother's arm, steered her away from the food court, back toward the mall's main concourse.

"I guess I changed my mind."

"Well," Joyce said after a moment. Then her expression brightened. Buffy had a flash of intuition that told her what was coming next. Her mom was going to try for a "with it" moment. "They do say that's a woman's prerogative."

Buffy gave her mother's arm a pat. "Nice try, Mom. But I think you need to do a millennium check."

It was Saturday afternoon, not the time the world was usually treated to the sight of teenage girls shopping with their mothers. But when Joyce had asked Buffy if she'd like to run a few quick errands with her, if she didn't have any other plans, that is, Buffy had opened her mouth and surprised them both by saying the opposite of no.

The truth was, things had been really good lately in the Summers household. Not so good that Buffy was afraid her mom was going to start looking for matching mother-daughter dresses or sign them up for wreath-making classes. There were limits to the whole concept of teen-to-parent relationship goodness, after all.

But things at home were, well, sort of peaceful. A good sort of peaceful. At ease-and-full-of-acceptance-type peaceful. Not the sort of peace that turned out to be the lull before the bad-ass storm.

Buffy thought it had something to do with the Slayage action during the last few days, which was definitely at an all-time low. As a result, the Scooby Gang was sort of on hiatus. They still spent time together, sure, but each of them had also had more time than usual alone.

Since Buffy could hardly spend her time hanging out with Angel, not in the way she'd like to, anyway, sort of by default, she'd ended up at home. Last weekend, she and her mom had actually baked cookies and watched a movie together. This weekend, they were shopping at the mall.

Good-bye, Sunnydale. Hello, Pleasantville, Buffy thought, as she followed Joyce down a short side corridor of the mall. At the rate things were going, if Buffy wasn't careful, she'd have to pay a trip to the doctor to be innoculated against "Happy Days" Syndrome.

Though, when she was being honest with herself, she had to admit she felt okay about all this togetherness with her mom. It wasn't like they'd had so much of it Buffy could afford to take any of it for granted. Particularly since Slayers sometimes didn't live all that long.

As if on cue, Buffy's Slayer senses went on red alert. The hair stood up on the back of her neck and an ice-cold prickle shot down her spine.

"I just want to run in here for a minute and then we're done," Joyce said, oblivious to what Buffy was experiencing. "I need to pick up some more scrapbook supplies."

For the first time, Buffy noticed their location. They were standing outside a card store.

Whoa, Buffy thought, her Slayer senses still announcing some potentially hostile presence. *Kind of a strong reaction to way-too-cute greeting cards.*

Though there was always the possibility that Buffy's reaction had been brought on by her own feelings about her mom's little cut-and-paste project. For the last week or so, Joyce had spent every spare moment putting together a scrapbook about Buffy. She claimed it was a retrospective, something to celebrate Buffy's many achievements, bridge the gap between child and adulthood.

Buffy appreciated the thought. She really did. There were just two teeny-weeny problems. The first was that most of her really big accomplishments could never be caught on film. The second was that, given the life span of the average Slayer, Buffy's mom's project got her own personal vote for most likely to end up as a Buffy Summers memorial.

"You go ahead, Mom," she said now, trying to determine what had really caused her reaction by casing the walkway around them in a way that she hoped wasn't too obvious. "I'll just sort of stay out here and do the teen thing. You know, loiter."

Joyce's forehead creased. "Is anything wrong, Buffy?"

"No, no," Buffy said, giving her mother her perkiest smile. Her Slayer's baddie beacon was busy homing in on a figure staring into the display window a couple of stores down. *Gotcha,* Buffy thought. Nobody who wore that much leather could possibly be into bean-bag dolls.

Oh yeah. Something was definitely going on.

Buffy didn't think it was vamp action. It was the middle of the day, after all. But vamps weren't the only monsters who liked to show their ugly mugs in Sunnydale, a fact that, as the Slayer, Buffy knew all too well and to her cost.

"You go ahead, Mom, really," she urged. "I don't mind waiting out here, but I don't think I can handle going in. I just don't feel all that warm and fuzzy right now."

"Well, all right," Joyce agreed, her tone reluctant. "If you say so. I'll only be a minute, sweetheart. By the way," she continued, her voice dropping to a whisper, "that girl down there—the one making the rather unfortunate fashion choices? She's been following us ever since we left the food court."

Impressed, Buffy gave her mother's arm another pat, this time an approving one. "Way to use your Spidey senses, Mom. Not to worry, however. Situation under control. Run along now."

Her mother hesitated for another moment, her eyes fixed on Buffy. Buffy could almost read her thoughts. Feel her reluctance to leave her only daughter in anything that might resemble danger—her desire to take a stand beside her, protect her at all costs.

She also knew the exact moment her mother changed her mind.

Joyce's mouth twisted wryly, the corners pulling down. *And just want did you think you'd be able to do?* that mouth said. *You're only the mother of the Slayer, after all.*

She opened her mouth, then closed it again. Buffy felt her heart squeeze just once. And answered the question her mom had decided not to ask.

"I promise I'll be careful, Mom."

The corners of Joyce's mouth turned up, ever so slightly. Then she turned and walked into the store. Buffy waited until her mom had disappeared behind a display of cookie tins with angel teddy bears on them before she went into action. She sprinted to the far end of the corridor.

There was a set of bathrooms back there, if she had her mall geography right, and she was pretty sure she did. The only place she'd ever had occasion to use what few geography skills she actually possessed was at the mall.

She whipped around the corner, relieved to find the short hallway by the bathrooms empty, and cast a quick glance above her. Overhead was a very large light. The mall had undergone a remodel recently, due to that unfortunate incident with a rocket launcher. As a result, all the light fixtures were new. This one was a sort of retro chandelier.

Perfect, Buffy thought. Without hesitation, she bent

her knees and jumped. She'd just finished swinging her legs up out of the way when a figure in black leather hurtled around the corner, then stopped short. She looked back over her shoulder once, then headed straight for the women's bathroom, smacking both palms against the door.

Buffy felt her bicep muscles tighten as she counted to about a hundred. That's how long it took for the other girl to come bursting back out the door. She skidded to an abrupt stop, staring at the door to the guy's bathroom. Buffy gave it an even fifty-fifty.

She waited until the girl had actually turned, plainly having decided to enter the inner sanctum, before she let herself drop to the floor. If this girl wanted Buffy badly enough and was willing to go into a guy's bathroom to find her, it was definitely time to find out why.

"Looking for someone?" asked the Slayer.

Dropping into a fighting crouch, the girl spun around. Instantly, Buffy went into a defensive posture, weight balanced over the balls of her feet. There was a charged silence, as the two girls stared at one another. Buffy did a quick catalog.

The girl before her was definitely dressed to intimidate. She was wearing enough leather to guarantee a Hall of Fame spot on the People for the Ethical Treatment of Animals hit list. A silver stud sprouted from the right side of her nose. Another protruded from the middle of her lower lip.

Heavy silver rings wrapped almost every finger. Who needed brass knuckles when you could make fashion choices like those? About the only part of her that didn't have some piece of metal wrapped around it or protruding from it were her ears, somewhat to Buffy's surprise.

The other surprise was that, now that she'd gotten a good look at her, Buffy realized that she knew who this was.

It was a girl from school named Suz Tompkins. Suz ran with the toughest crowd there was at Sunnydale High. Actually, about half of Suz's friends no longer bothered to come to classes. They just showed up on campus to look bad and hang out.

Finding Suz Tompkins at the Sunnydale Mall on a Saturday was strange, to say the least. About as likely as . . . finding Buffy Summers there with her mom.

Buffy straightened up. "You skipped ear piercing, Suz."

Noting the change in Buffy's posture, Suz Tompkins straightened up, too. She gave Buffy a wolfish smile.

"I'm thinking of having my lobes stretched," she answered.

"Tribal," Buffy replied. She cocked her head, as if considering. "I don't know, though. Could be a liability in close quarters. Perfect thing to grab onto in a fight."

"Good point," Suz conceded. "I'll keep it in mind." Her eyes watched Buffy for a moment. "I've heard you're good in a fight," she went on.

Her tone of voice was so deliberately neutral that Buffy knew she'd just been given the answer to at least part of the reason Suz Tompkins had gone to so much trouble to find her. The question was, did she want to ask for Buffy's help, or did she want to try to take her down? A sort of Sunnydale version of gunslinger syndrome. Buffy'd encountered it from time to time.

She knew her Slayer strength and skills would give her a definite edge, but she still felt a second shiver ease down her spine. In spite of her tough tone, Suz wasn't acting like somebody about to issue a challenge. That was just the way she sounded all the time.

But if Suz wanted Buffy's help, the situation must be major. Buffy couldn't imagine anybody wanting to tangle with Suz Tompkins. At least, nobody in their right mind.

The guy's bathroom door swung open, whacking Suz Tompkins in the back, before Buffy could ask what was going on. Instantly, Suz shifted so that she could see who was coming out at the same time she kept an eye on Buffy. Buffy noticed the way the other girl kept her back to the wall. Suz Tompkins wasn't taking any chances, not even in the middle of the day at the Sunnydale Mall.

And if that wasn't an interesting little factoid, Buffy Summers didn't know what was.

"What are you looking at?" Suz snarled.

The guy emerging from the bathroom looked like the white rabbit from *Alice in Wonderland*. His Adam's apple bobbed up and down when he swallowed. And looking at Suz Tompkins was making him swallow a lot.

"N-nothing," he stammered, as he scooted between Suz and Buffy. He scurried to the end of the corridor, then vanished around the corner. Buffy could practically see his little white tail disappearing down the rabbit hole.

"That's quite a way with people you've got," she observed.

"It's a gift," Suz Tompkins said shortly. "Look, Buffy, I—I'm sorry about the stalker bit, but I really need to talk to you about something."

"I'm all ears," Buffy said.

But Suz Tompkins was already shaking her head. "Not here. All this swimming in the mainstream is making me sick to my stomach."

"Where, then?" Buffy asked. "And when?"

"Tonight," Suz Tompkins answered. "I'll meet you at the Bronze."

CHAPTER 3

"Tell me why we're doing this again?" Willow shouted.

It was about nine o'clock on Saturday night, and things were just starting to heat up at the Bronze.

Bodies gyrated wildly on the dance floor to the sounds of Dingoes Ate My Baby. Because the noise level was loud enough to make conversation difficult, Willow had spent most of her evening staring adoringly at Oz. Xander'd kept an eagle-eye on the door watching for Cordelia, in spite of the fact that her arrival was only likely to make him miserable.

Just another Sunnydale Saturday night.

Buffy had divided her time between doing her best to convince herself she'd chosen to sit at one of the tables with the tall stools because it would be easier for Suz Tompkins to spot her—it had *nothing* to do with the fact that she was hoping to spot Angel—and trying not to stress over what was happening between her and her mom.

Joyce had accepted Buffy's explanation of the girl in black leather as a schoolmate in trouble without comment, almost as if she'd made a promise to herself not to interfere while she'd been shopping in that card store. Instead of pumping Buffy for information, she'd talked enthusiastically about the scrapbook project all the way home from the mall.

She'd given Buffy her own space for the rest of the day, not even asking her to set the table for dinner, which they'd had together. She'd been happily pasting pictures of Buffy at about age ten into the scrapbook and watching a Cary Grant movie on TV when Buffy departed for the Bronze.

Things were so good that Buffy was starting to worry. Could the fact that she and her mom were getting along so well actually be an indication that something was terribly wrong? Not seeing eye-to-eye with your parents was supposed to be what being a teenager was all about, wasn't it?

Buffy wasn't obsessing about this, was she?

Oh, no. Definitely not.

"What did you say?" she shouted back at Willow.

"I said—" Willow began. A resounding crash of cymbals from the Dingoes Ate My Baby drummer drowned her out completely. "—tell me why we're doing this again," she shouted at the top of her lungs.

Heads turned all over the Bronze.

The cymbal crash had marked the end of the Dingoes' set. Willow's sense of social timing defied description. Par for the course. Every single person in the Bronze had heard her shouted question.

As she realized what had happened, Willow's face turned a shade that Buffy was sure the fashion consultants for *Young Miss* magazine would feel obliged to point out did not go well with the color of Willow's hair. Redheads weren't supposed to wear red, after all. Fortunately for her, Xander was prepared to be her knight in shining armor.

If there was anyone who knew what it felt like to be embarrassed in public, it was Xander Harris.

He stood up, blocking Willow from as much view as he could.

"Pay no attention to the woman behind the green corduroy."

The faces that went with the heads smirked, then turned away. Willow's twenty seconds of fame were over.

"Dug the set, huh?" Oz said as he materialized beside her.

"Oz, no!" Willow stuttered, her head appearing over the top of Xander's shoulder. "It was nothing like that. I promise."

"You might want to consider a retake on that one, Will," Buffy advised.

Xander sat back down. Now that Oz was here, he could take over knight duty. There was a certain hierarchy to teen relationships, after all.

"But, wait," Willow choked out. "Time out. Start over. Set good. Timing bad."

Oz nodded. "That's cool," he said.

"Cleared things up for me," Buffy put in.

"So—what is this thing we're doing?" Oz asked.

Oz's ability to focus under virtually every circumstance was one of the things Buffy liked best about him. That and his hair, of course.

"We're waiting for Suz Tompkins."

Oz's bushy eyebrows rose. "Suz Tompkins. Major."

"There!" Willow said, as if Oz had just proved her point.

"Majorly major," Xander seconded. "Which is why the Scooby Gang has been called in." Without missing a beat, he launched into the theme song. "Scooby Dooby Do, I see—whoa—big trouble in little Sunnydale."

"Xander," Willow protested. "That's not the way it goes."

"No, I mean it," Xander said. "And it's headed straight for us."

Quickly, Buffy looked toward the entrance to the Bronze. The crowd was busy parting like the Red Sea to reveal Cordelia, with Suz Tompkins looking like she was permanently attached to one arm. The look on Cordelia's face would have curdled fresh milk.

While it was still inside the cow.

"Now that is definitely a sight you don't see every day," Oz observed.

"Suz Tompkins looks kind of funny," Willow commented.

"I think the word you're looking for is terrified, Will," Buffy said.

"Wouldn't you be?" asked Oz.

Like a battleship under full steam, Cordelia plowed her way through the Bronze. When she reached Buffy's table, she gave her arm an angry shake.

"All right, we're here. Now do you *mind?*"

Suz Tompkins let go of Cordelia's arm. The second she was free of the other girl's grasp, Cordelia immediately began to inspect the sleeve of her silk blouse.

"If your grubby youth-at-risk paws have ruined this, you're buying me a new one," she informed Suz Tompkins.

Now that she was actually standing at Buffy's table, Suz Tompkins appeared to have recovered somewhat. She no longer looked white with terror, just green around the gills. Though Buffy had to admit that could just be the lighting in the Bronze.

"Blue light special at K-Mart, right?" Suz asked.

"In your wildest dreams," Cordelia answered. "Don't confuse my shopping habits with your own. Oh, my God, I think that's a sweat mark." She held her arm up for the rest of the table to examine. "Do you see what that candidate for being tried as an adult has done?"

Xander slid off his stool, determined to head off trouble. "Cordelia, why don't you let me get you something?"

"What a truly fabulous idea," Cordelia said. "How about a tetanus shot?"

Xander grabbed for her hand. Cordelia yanked it back.

"How many times do I have to tell you not to touch me in public?" she said. But she followed Xander toward the bar.

Suz watched them go, her expression stony. "And you guys put up with that because . . . ?"

Right, Buffy thought. *Dissing my friends is so the best way to ask for my help.*

"I think it's something called friendship," she said quietly. "Ring any bells?"

Suz Tompkins sucked in a breath, and changed right before Buffy's astonished eyes.

Suz's face crumpled, as if she was in pain. Her shoulders slumped. Tears filled her heavily-lined eyes. Plainly, Buffy's words had gone in deep.

"Drink?" Oz asked Willow softly.

Willow slid from her stool, her hand in his. The two slipped into the crowd, leaving Buffy and Suz Tompkins alone. Suz hesitated, as if uncertain what to do next. Buffy nodded toward Willow's empty stool.

"Sit down."

Suz eased herself onto the stool, still obviously struggling for control. Buffy considered the best way to get the ball rolling, wishing she didn't feel quite so much like a guidance counselor. This was not the sort of reaching out and touching someone at which she excelled.

"So, Suz," she said. "What's going on?"

"It's about my friends," Suz started, then broke off. She pressed her lips together tightly, as if she was afraid that she'd start to sob right there in the middle of the Bronze.

Okay, Buffy thought. She could play twenty questions if that's what it took. She liked questions. Questions were good. As long as they weren't of the math-test variety.

"You think they're in trouble?" she prompted.

This time, Suz Tompkins really did sob. Just once. A harsh, desperate, lonely sound. In the next instant, she'd pulled in a deep breath, gotten herself back under control.

"You could say that," she said, her tortured eyes meeting Buffy's across the table. "I think they're dying."

CHAPTER 4

In the big white house that sat alone on the hill above the town, Webster and Percy were preparing to be naughty little vampire boys.

Their Mama had warned them about their wilder tendencies. She'd advised her sons not to give in to them. They'd been brought up better than that, after all. One of the marks of a true gentleman was that he never let his baser instincts control him.

But Mama was also the first to admit that Webster and Percy's sudden impulses to disobey her were only natural. It was something to do with how old they'd been when they'd been changed. How old—or young— they'd always be. Fifteen. An age swayed by surging hormones.

Webster and Percy weren't all that sure they really had hormones anymore, whatever those were. But if they knew anything, they knew that there were times when it was better not to argue with their mama.

Mama had warned them about something else, too, just that night. She'd warned them not to hunt again too soon. Things were good in Sunnydale, the best they'd been in a long time. There was no sense being greedy and spoiling it all.

Webster and Percy had nodded, to show they understood. But even as they'd done so, they'd been making plans of their own. They'd already found their next victim. In fact, they'd been stalking her for almost a week now. They'd even let her catch a glimpse of them, once or twice. Not enough to get a really good look. Just enough so that she'd know this feeling that somebody was out to get her was the real thing. That her mind wasn't playing tricks on her. Something else was.

Percy and Webster had come to enjoy the way the girl had started to look over her shoulder. The way they'd made her afraid to walk the streets alone. They figured she'd run long and fast, fueled by her own fear. All they could think about was finishing things off, hunting her down.

They didn't want to wait. Didn't see the need to wait. Well, Mama'd said it herself, hadn't she?

Boys will be boys.

"Come on, Webster," Percy whispered, as he stuck his leg out their bedroom window and prepared to climb down a convenient apple tree. "Let's go see what's come out to play."

Behind him, Webster gave a high-pitched giggle.

"Besides us, of course."

Buffy'd gotten Suz Tompkins a glass of water, then watched in amazement as the other girl took one long drink, fished a piece of Kleenex from her pocket, dunked it, and used the soggy tissue to wipe off her eyeliner. Without her make-up Suz looked a lot younger. And much more vulnerable.

"So, what do you think is happening?" Buffy asked. She pitched her voice low.

In the time it had taken Buffy to get Suz's drink, a second band had taken over from the Dingoes. Of the striving-to-be-socially-relevant variety. On the Bronze's stage, a bass player backed a lanky girl as she whispered into a hand-held microphone. Her face was completely obscured by a curtain of long, dark hair. Buffy had no idea what she looked like.

"I don't know for sure," Suz answered. Her naked eyelids looked red and puffy. "Nothing I can prove anyway. I just know that something's wrong and I've got no one to talk to about it. I mean, it's not like I'm going to find a lot of people lining up to be all worried. You've probably noticed I don't exactly hang with the merit scholar crowd."

"Me neither," Buffy said.

"What about Rosenberg?" Suz countered. "I've heard she's a walking four-oh."

"Well, she is," Buffy agreed. "And though my math skills may not be the best, even I can figure out that it takes more than one to make a crowd."

Suz relaxed enough to give a snort of laughter and picked up the glass of water. It was halfway to her lips before she remembered the contents now probably qualified as hazardous waste. She set the glass down again, abruptly. Water sloshed over the rim and onto the table.

Buffy pushed the soda she'd been drinking across the table toward her. "Nothing contagious, I promise."

Suz took a sip, set the glass down, then used the straw to jab at the ice cubes. Watching her, Buffy had a sudden out of body moment. She figured this must be exactly how her mother felt when trying to get important information out of her. Information she'd really rather keep to herself, even though she knew she shouldn't.

"Come on, Suz," Buffy said, trying to match the concerned yet no-nonsense tone her mother always adopted on such occasions. "You're stalling and you know it."

"It's just I feel so stupid!" Suz burst out. "You're going to think I'm nuts or something."

"I won't," Buffy said. If there was one thing she'd learned since becoming the Slayer, it was that absolutely nothing was impossible. There *were* things that went bump in the night, and Buffy had gotten up close and personal with most of them. If a girl as tough as Suz Tompkins was scared, there was probably a very good reason for it.

"It happened the first time about a month ago," Suz said haltingly. "Leila Johns just disappeared. Heidi— Heidi Lindstrom, my best friend—she and Leila and I were supposed to go to a movie or something. But Leila never showed, and then she didn't show for school the next morning. She never really went to class much anyway, so I don't think the teachers even noticed."

Suz paused and took another sip of Buffy's soda.

"Did you talk to anybody about it?" Buffy asked.

"What about Leila's family? Don't they know where she's gone?"

Suz shook her head. "I tried," she answered. "But I'm not exactly on the best of speaking terms with Leila's mom. She thinks I'm a bad influence or something."

Or something. "How about the police?" Buffy persisted. "Did you file a missing persons report?"

On stage, the singer abruptly let out a burst of wild laughter. Suz Tompkins joined her.

"Get real," she said shortly. "Look at me, Buffy. The cops have the same opinion of me as your friend Cordelia and Leila's mom. They take one look and see a felony in progress. I tell the cops I'm worried 'cause one of my friends didn't make a movie date, and I guarantee you they'll laugh so hard they'll ralph up their morning doughnuts."

Buffy wrinkled her nose in disgust. *There are some things even a Slayer shouldn't be forced to confront.*

"Couldn't Leila have just gone off somewhere and not told you guys about it?"

Before Buffy'd even finished her sentence, Suz Tompkins was shaking her head from side to side.

"She wouldn't have done that," she said, her tone rising.

"Why not?"

Suz's face flushed an angry red. "Because she's not like that!" she all but shouted.

"Will you be quiet?" a guy at the next table broke in. "I can't hear the band."

Suz turned toward him. Buffy thought the other girl actually bared her teeth. "Back off," she said.

Without another word, the guy picked up his drink and chose another table. Suz turned back.

"Impressive," Buffy commented.

"I knew you wouldn't believe me," Suz accused. "You're just like all the others. You only see what you want to see."

"I only see what you let me see, Suz," Buffy countered. "If you want me to see more, you'll have to show me where to look."

Way to go, pop psychology.

Suz Tompkins put her head down in her hands. Her shoulders slumped. All the fight seemed to go right out of her. Buffy was surprised to feel a funny lump form in the back of her throat. She knew what despair looked like when she saw it.

"I don't know if you can understand this . . . but . . . my friends and I . . . we have have . . . rules," Suz finally said softly.

"Nobody does anything major, anything that could impact the group, without letting everybody else know about it. It's the way we protect ourselves, you know? Watch our own backs. Take care of one another. Leila would never take off without saying something. None of us would. Don't ask me to explain how I know for sure, I just do. *I know it, Buffy.*"

"That's why you think she's dead. She didn't say that she was going, and she hasn't been in touch."

Suz Tompkins nodded. She began to fiddle with the straw again, her body tense, as if expecting Buffy to make another denial at any moment. When Buffy didn't offer one, Suz's hands grew still. Buffy frowned in concentration, staring absently out across the crowded Bronze, her mind turning over the pieces of Suz's puzzle.

While it was true that not every bad thing that happened in Sunnydale had a direct link to the Hellmouth, Buffy knew better than to start out by assuming that the Hellmouth *wasn't* involved. On the other hand, it was possible, theoretically at any rate, that Leila Johns could have been done away with by perfectly normal, not very nice guys.

But what if she hadn't been? What if Buffy'd been lulled into a false sense of security thinking how quiet things had been lately, when really they hadn't been so quiet after all?

Some things that came out of the Hellmouth just wanted to wreak some havoc and then slink off again. Not everything wanted the Slayer to know it was in town.

She'd heard rumors of Leila's disappearance, Buffy realized now. She just hadn't paid all that much attention. Maybe Suz was right about her. Maybe she was just like everyone else. All those grown-ups who assumed that because a girl like Leila looked like trouble, when she met trouble she deserved what she got, had found what she was looking for.

Abruptly, Buffy's eyes focused and she realized what she'd been staring at all this time. Intuitively, her gaze had gone straight to where Willow was helping Oz pack up the Dingoes' sound equipment. Xander and Cordy stood nearby. Not that Cordelia was doing anything to help, of course.

Now that she was paying attention, Buffy could see that Willow kept glancing her way, trying to figure out what was going on.

Buffy knew what people thought when they saw her group together. They were the freaks and geeks. With the exception of Cordelia, the misfits of Sunnydale High.

Those are my *friends,* she thought. Her friends, who'd proved more times than she could count that they would do literally anything for her. *We have rules, too,* she realized.

And first on the list was that friends never broke their own rules, never broke the promises they'd made to one another. Friends kept their word. They stuck together no matter what. . . .

"I'm not going back over there," Cordelia announced. "You can't make me. So just forget about it."

Oz snapped the lock on his guitar case closed. "Looks heavy," he commented.

"Well, if you had a *real* band, you wouldn't have to carry it yourself. You'd have, you know, groupies, or something."

Cordelia became the focus of three pairs of eyes. "What?" She sat up a little straighter, alarm plain in her face. "I don't have something in my teeth, do I?"

"I think he was talking about Buffy and Suz," Willow finally said quietly. During Oz's take-down, she'd continued to watch Buffy's table from across the room, her expression both worried and thoughtful.

"How come we never learn anything useful in school?" she complained. "Like lip reading or something?"

"If Buffy's going to get involved with somebody like Suz Tompkins, she can count me out," Cordelia went on. "I absolutely draw the line."

"And a straight and narrow one it is, too," Xander spoke up.

Cordelia glared. "Could you be more annoying?"

Xander smiled. "That's for me to know and you to find out," he said.

"Don't bother," Cordelia snapped back. "I already know."

Buffy pulled her attention away from her friends. She had a job to do, and she couldn't accomplish it by going all greeting-card sappy.

"Who else is missing?" she asked Suz Tompkins.

Suz stared at her across the table. Slowly, Buffy watched the realization dawn in the other girl's eyes.

"You believe me, don't you?" Suz asked.

"I believe you," Buffy answered softly. "But you said 'friends,' Suz. Plural, as in more than one. That must mean somebody else is missing, too. Who is it?"

Suz's eyes filled with tears once more. Buffy felt her stomach twist. She forced herself not to look back over toward Willow. Because she knew what Suz was going to say, this time.

"Last week—" Suz said. Her voice came out rough and ragged. She cleared her throat, tried again. "Last week, it was my best friend, Heidi Lindstrom."

Webster and Percy were experiencing something of a letdown.

They'd been roaming the streets for over an hour now, and they still hadn't found the girl they'd chosen. Webster was all for calling it quits and heading for home. Mama had probably realized that they were gone by now.

And the truth was that there were occasions when Mama had embarrassed her darling boys. She'd been known to come looking for them when they went hunting without asking her permission first. When they struck out on their own and conveniently forgot that the rules she made were for their own good.

Life was really so much easier when Mama was happy, Webster reminded Percy. But Percy wasn't ready to call it a night. Not quite yet. Uh uh.

There was someplace Percy wanted to go first. The place he was almost certain the girl would go. The same place they'd found the last one. Only this time, Percy wanted more. He didn't want to wait in the back alley to see what came out. This time, Percy wanted to go inside, where the prey, where the action was.

It would mean they'd have to wear their human faces, which was a bore. But even Percy knew better than to go into a crowded place in full vamp mode. If Mama ever found out they'd done that, she'd have an absolute conniption for sure. Definitely something Percy wanted to avoid.

"It has a funny name," he said to Webster, as he took him by the arm to hurry him along. Sometimes, Webster was so slow it annoyed and embarrassed Percy. It reflected poorly on him. They were twins, after all. "A metal name."

"Gold," Webster suggested.

"That's not it," Percy said, steering his brother around a corner and up a darkened street.

"Silver."

"That's not it, either."

"Copper."

"No," Percy said impatiently, bringing Webster to an abrupt halt with a jerk on his arm.

"Percy," Webster whined. "You're being a bully, *and* you're being rude. If you don't start being nicer to me right this minute, I'm telling Mama when we get home."

"We're here, Webster," Percy said. He released his brother's arm and pointed.

"I was going to guess that next," Webster said.

The sign above the front door said, BRONZE.

It had taken some fast talking and another soda, but Buffy had finally convinced Suz to let the others rejoin them. Appealing to Suz's sense of friendship had finally tipped the scales. That and the fact that Cordelia had bailed. If Suz trusted Buffy, she was going to have to trust Buffy's friends, too. Those were *her* rules.

Once they were all reassembled, Buffy'd filled her friends in, quickly. When she was finished, Suz had signaled her acceptance of the fact that the others were now involved by adding one final piece of information.

She was pretty sure her number was up next. Because she was absolutely sure that she was being followed. The stalking had started right after Heidi had disappeared.

Oz was the first to speak up. "Did you see who it was?" he asked quietly. Not that he ever asked any other kind of way.

"Not really," answered Suz Tompkins. "You know, not enough so that I could identify them in a police line-up. Just enough to give me the creeps."

Her forehead wrinkled, as if she was trying to remember details. "I think they dressed kind of funny."

Willow choked on a mouthful of soda. Suz turned toward her.

"All the time?" Willow hurried into speech.

"How should I know?" Suz asked. "I don't help them get dressed in the morning."

"No, I mean, do you feel like you're being *followed* all the time," Willow clarified. "Or is it, you know, only certain times. Like, say, for instance, after dark."

Suz considered, her face thoughtful. If she noticed the way the tension at the table had just ratcheted up a notch, she didn't show it.

"Only after dark," she confirmed after a moment.

Well, Buffy thought. *That definitely narrows down the list of suspects.* There were lots of things that didn't like to get a tan, but only a few for whom those UV rays would prove instantly fatal from a case of spontaneous combustion.

And topping the list . . .

"Hey," a new voice said.

"Oh. Wow. Look. It's Angel," Willow squeaked. "I mean, you know, what good—"

"Timing," Xander finished for her.

Angel looked from one to the other, his eyes narrowing slightly.

He'd long since become accustomed to the fact that the reception he received from Buffy's nearest and dearest could, and often did, vary nightly. Not that he cared about it for himself. Not much. But Angel didn't like being a source of conflict between Buffy and her friends. He figured just being the Slayer was hard enough on her. Particularly since it included the whole evil-Angel-tried-to-kill-her-and-everyone-she-loved thing.

Actually, so far, all things considered, tonight's response was pretty positive.

"You guys have been practicing again, right?" he asked.

As usual, it was Willow who responded. Xander only dealt with Angel directly when he didn't like his other options. Say, for instance, in cases when his imminent demise seemed highly likely.

Willow nodded. "Night and day. And day and night."

"That should cover it," Angel said dryly.

How does he do it? Buffy wondered. His presence always jolted her. And, no matter how hard she tried to be prepared, the moment she least expected him was bound to be the one when he showed up.

But then, the truth was, she'd never really been prepared for Angel. How did a girl get ready to deal with the fact that her soulmate was a vampire over 200 years old?

He moved to stand beside her, though he didn't touch her. He rarely did, in front of others.

"Angel, this is Suz. Suz, Angel," Buffy performed the necessary introductions.

"Hey," Angel said.

"Hey," Suz answered.

"Well," Xander said, as if unable to resist the chance to needle. "I can certainly feel my heartstrings being plucked by that touching little moment."

Angel ignored him. "Buffy," he said, his gaze prowling the Bronze restlessly. "We need to talk. I—"

"Oh, my God. I think that's them," said Suz Tompkins.

Every head at the table swiveled in the direction Suz was pointing. After a moment, Buffy could see two guys making their way through the Bronze.

They were dressed exactly alike in khaki pants and white button-down oxford cloth shirts. The only thing that marked one from the other were their ties. One navy blue. One maroon. Buffy couldn't see their feet, but she was willing to bet her virtually nonexistent college fund on penny loafers. With the pennies actually in them.

The guys were rubbernecking, seemingly oblivious to the stares and snickers going on around them, craning their necks as if to take in every single detail of the Bronze. They looked exactly like five-year-olds who'd just been turned loose in a candy store. Without adult supervision.

When they spotted Suz, the two guys began to whisper together. The one in the navy blue tie actually waved. Maroon-tie slaped his arm down.

"That's them?" Xander asked, his tone incredulous. He turned to look at Suz Tompkins. "You're afraid of the Pillsbury Doughboys? Why didn't you just poke them in their little tummies or something?"

"Xander," Buffy said warningly.

"What?" Xander said. "It's a reasonable question. Inquiring minds want to know."

"You're right," Willow told Suz. "They do dress funny."

"Out of date," Angel put in.

Xander snorted. "Like you'd know." Then his expression changed, as if a new thought had suddenly occurred to him.

"Wait for it," Oz said. "Here it comes."

"Hold it a second," Xander went on, all his attention now on Angel. "Are you trying to say you *recognize* those guys?"

"Never seen 'em before," Angel said calmly, "though you could say I'm . . . familiar with the type." His dark eyes sought Buffy's. "I'm willing to bet these are new kids in town."

"Well, then," Buffy said, sliding from her stool to stand beside him. "I'd say a warm Sunnydale welcome is in order."

"What are you guys talking about?" whined Suz Tompkins.

Ten minutes later, Buffy and Angel were in the alley behind the Bronze. Not that it had taken that long to come up with their plan of attack, which was pretty straightforward:

1. Locate twin vamps.
2. Dust 'em.
3. Call it a night and head for home.

But ten minutes was how long it had taken Buffy to convince Suz to let her handle things, while Oz and Willow drove her home with Xander sort of riding shotgun. After that, the Scooby Gang would proceed to the school library to rendezvous with Buffy and do a check-in with Giles.

Now that she'd gotten a good look at her two supposed stalkers, much of Suz's fear had vanished. She was all for taking them out herself. Right here. Right now. After she'd done whatever it took to make them tell her what they'd done to Leila and Heidi. Buffy didn't bother to explain how different the torture would be in this case.

"Suz does have a point," Buffy said, as she and Angel moved cautiously down the alley. The guys hadn't looked very tough, but Buffy was the expert on how appearances could be deceiving. She already had a stake drawn.

"Which is?" Angel said.

"We should at least try to confirm whether or not these guys were responsible for whatever happened to Heidi and Leila."

"Okay," Angel said. "You tickle them till they spill the beans. I'll hold 'em down."

Buffy sighed. "You've been watching the cartoon network again, haven't you?"

"I have to do something all day. I get bored."

"Try attending Sunnydale High."

"Oooh, look, Webster," said a voice behind them.

With Angel pivoting with perfect precision beside her, Buffy spun around. Behind them were the twins from the Bronze, the fitful glow of the Bronze's back door light reflecting off their beady little yellow eyes. The boys were in vamp mode, reverting to their true colors now that they weren't really out in public anymore.

"Well, well," Angel murmured. "Able to leap tall buildings in a single bound."

He could have sworn the alley behind them had been empty just a moment before. He'd checked. Angel was good at things like that. He knew what made a difference, after all.

"I told you this was going to be our lucky night," said the one in the maroon tie. "Two for the price of one."

"I don't know, Percy," navy blue tie said nervously. "You know Mama doesn't like it when we take on even odds."

"What are you gonna do? Tell on me?" Percy taunted.

"You're not supposed to talk to me like that!" the vamp named Webster wailed. "Mama said so."

"Mama's boys," Angel said in disgust. "I hate mamas' boys."

Buffy elbowed him in the stomach. "I hate it when you steal all my best lines."

"Sorry," Angel said.

"You can make it up to me," Buffy suggested with a quick bat of her eyes.

"How?"

Buffy raised her arm. "Help me introduce Tweedledum and Tweedledee here to Mr. Pointy."

Angel's devil-may-care grin flashed out. Buffy felt her pulse kick up a notch.

"You're on," Angel promised. "It's my turn to count, though."

"You only ever go to three," Buffy mock-complained.

"One . . . Two . . ." Angel said.

In perfect harmony, perfect rhythm, the Slayer and the vampire lunged forward.

I only posed? he *No, mine,* she thought.

She was right. It wasn't. Terry and Webster, when both Buffy and Angel were almost on them. Then they ducked forward.

Buffy reacted on instinct, shoving the stake up the sleeve of her jacket and dropping to her back on the pavement of the alley, the air whooshing from her lungs as she went down, hard. She tried her right leg, bent like a familiar at the elbow, and caught the vamp in the solar plexus with her foot, smash to the stomach.

As he began to double over, she caught his ankle,

CHAPTER 5

Webster wailed like a blubbering banshee, but he and Percy held their ground. For one beat of the Slayer's accelerated heart, it appeared to Buffy that all she and Angel were going to have to do was walk right up and stake the twin twerps through their black little vampire hearts.

It can't possibly be this easy, she thought.

She was right. It wasn't. Percy and Webster waited until Buffy and Angel were almost on them. Then they, too, rushed forward.

Buffy reacted on instinct, shoving the stake up the sleeve of her jacket and dropping to her back on the pavement of the alley, the air whooshing from her lungs as she went down hard. She lifted her right leg, knee bent like a tumbler at the circus, and caught the vamp in the maroon tie with her foot, square in the stomach.

As he began to double over, she caught his wrists,

then used his own momentum to pitch him over. Beside her, she heard Angel give a grunt of exertion and knew he was accomplishing the same thing, though she didn't look to see quite how.

As soon as the vamp cleared, Buffy vaulted to her feet and whipped around. By the time she'd completed her turn, the stake was back in her fist, in the ready position once more. Buffy wasn't about to leave her back exposed, not even for an instant. Especially not to a vampire in penny loafers.

Once more, the four stared at each other.

"Oooh, that was fun, wasn't it?" the vamp in the maroon tie asked, his fangs gleaming as he grinned. "Didn't you think that was fun, Webster?"

"He got my shirt dirty," Webster said. Buffy had to admit she was impressed. So few individuals, dead or alive, could glare and sulk all at the same time. "Let's get out of here, Percy. I want to go home."

"Well, that makes one of you smarter than you look," Angel commented.

Webster poked his bottom lip out. "You're mean," he said. "I don't think I like you. And you definitely shouldn't talk to me like that. Mama wouldn't like it. If she finds out about it, there's no telling what she might do."

"I think I'll risk it," Angel said.

"Oh, but we're plenty smart, aren't we, Webster?" Percy broke in, grabbing his brother by the arm to silence him. "To prove it, let's all take this little quiz. Two of us can escape anytime we want to. Two of us are caught like rats in a trap. Which one's which?"

It was true, Buffy realized. The exchange of position

had given the vamps a potential advantage. They had the mouth of the alley open behind them while Buffy and Angel were backed by a dead end. Cornered. Rats. Trap. Pretty accurate description. Not that Buffy was going to reveal that, of course. *Over my dead body.*

Or, preferably, theirs.

"Come over here and I'll give you the answer," she challenged.

"You've got spunk," Percy commented with a grin. "I like that. You don't look quite right, of course. But I'm willing to be flexible, considering the circumstances."

Buffy could hardly believe her ears. Some vampire with the fashion sense of a fifties geek was dissing her sartorial selections? *Please.*

"You're telling me you choose your victims because of what they *look* like?" she asked, her tone incredulous. "You don't suppose that's shallow or anything."

"It isn't either shallow," Webster spoke up, his tone defensive. "Appearances are very important. You have to keep them up, no matter what. Mama says so."

"Your mother's first name wouldn't happen to be Martha, would it?" Buffy muttered.

"Are we done talking yet?" Angel suddenly asked. "'Cause, at the rate we're going, I'm thinking we might as well just get comfortable and wait for the sun to come up."

"Oh, no!" Webster squealed. "We can't do that. We can't let the sun touch us or we'll burn up."

Angel gave a snarl, morphing into vamp mode. "Tell me about it."

The twins jolted back a step. *Cheap shot, Angel,* Buffy thought.

"Wait a minute!" Webster wailed. "That's no fair. You're supposed to be on our side."

"I suggest you learn to deal real fast," Angel said. "Because I'm not. Stake me," he went on, extending one hand toward Buffy.

Without taking her eyes off the twins, the Slayer reached into her jacket pocket, produced a stake, and slapped it into Angel's outstretched palm.

"Don't hurt yourself with that," she warned.

"Trust me, I've got other plans. The whiner's mine."

"You can have him," Buffy promised. "All I want's a couple of minutes with fashion-consultant-boy."

She dropped into a fighter's crouch, tossing her stake from hand to hand, watching the way Percy followed it with his eyes.

"It's been fun," Angel said.

Webster simply turned and ran, with Angel right behind him. Buffy swore she heard one last cry of "Mama!" before the two disappeared around the end of the alley. She continued to toss the stake from hand to hand as she and Percy began to circle one another.

Buffy stayed low to the ground, her steps slow and gliding. Webster was a wimp, that much was plain. It was equally plain that Percy would fight like a wild animal when cornered. Much as she wanted to finish him off, Buffy knew better than to simply wade right in. Every instinct that she had was screaming at her that Percy would fight dirty.

She tossed the stake left. Abruptly, Percy feinted right, hoping to wrong-hand her, catch her off balance. It was exactly the kind of move Buffy'd been waiting for. The kind that would give her the opening she wanted.

She brought her right leg up in a swift cross-kick, catching the young vampire hard in the gut. Percy doubled over. Buffy raised her arm to knock him down with a blow to the back of the neck, but before she could land it, one of Percy's arms snaked out.

His fingers closed around the back of one of Buffy's knees, then viciously yanked forward. The joint buckled. Buffy went down. Percy scuttled backward out of range. He straightened as Buffy pushed herself to her feet. Again, the Slayer and the vampire circled one another, the stake in Buffy's hands a blur of motion.

Buffy's adrenaline was telling her to close in, to finish the job. But she forced herself to slow down. There was something she had to do first. Something she'd promised herself, and Suz Tompkins. She went back to throwing the stake in slow, even strokes. Left. Right. Right. Left.

"You're never going to be able to do this, you know," Percy said, as if he and Buffy were conversing at an afternoon tea party. "But if you give up now, I swear I'll make it quick."

"Right," Buffy nodded. "Dead guys. Living guys. You all make the same promises."

She could feel her pulse beating, quick and light. There was a funny taste in the back of her mouth, but she couldn't quite identify it.

"Well, what are you waiting for, sugar? I'm right here. Don't you want to finish me off?" Percy taunted.

Left. Right. Right. Left. Buffy watched Percy's eyes as they tried not to follow the stake. Knew her actions were starting to rattle and annoy him. Buffy grinned.

Rattling was good. And annoying. She really liked annoying.

"What do you think, bright boy?"

"I think you're not quite so brave without a big, strong guy beside you," Percy snapped, not quite so in control of himself now. "You're afraid a little girl like you won't be able to finish the job she started. Well, let me tell you something. You'd be right, honey."

Buffy tossed right, then tossed the stake end over end, the wood slapping as it hit the palm of her hand. End. Point. End. Point. *Die later. Die now. Die later. Die now.*

"Throwback. Vampire male chauvinist pig," she challenged.

"Oooh," Percy squealed. "You can talk dirty. I love it. I take back what I said before, when I said you weren't right for me. I think you're absolutely perfect, honey. Come on over here and let me prove it to you."

Abruptly, Buffy recognized the taste that filled her mouth. It was outrage. It was loathing. She wasn't a big vamp fan at the best of times, but this one was really something.

She supposed it was fair to say that Percy and his brother were just doing what vamps do, but they'd added a wrinkle Buffy definitely didn't care for. They'd deliberately targeted teenage girls. Chosen their victims because of what they looked like, if Buffy was getting the picture right.

Talk about fashion police. As if just being a female between the ages of twelve and twenty wasn't enough of a challenge.

Buffy gripped the end of the stake in her right hand,

weaving it in the air before her. *Die now. Any little minute now.*

"So that's how you picked those other two girls. It was just two, wasn't it?"

"Two down, you to go," Percy acknowledged.

"But why those girls?" Buffy asked. "Because of what they looked like? What'd they do, wear too much make-up?"

"They didn't look like ladies," Percy said. "The same way you don't. Ladies should be soft and feminine-looking. Mama says girls who don't are only good for one thing."

To be victims, Buffy thought. She felt the bitter taste flood her mouth. One long, thin finger of bile inched its way up the back of her throat. She swallowed it down.

Obviously, Percy's beloved mama had been letting him watch way too many retro slasher movies. Everybody knew looks-equals-death had gone out with *The Blob.*

"Funny," she said. "*My* mother always told me never to judge a book by its cover. But, in your case, I'm willing to make an exception."

"Ha ha. Very funny," Percy said. "Pardon me while I die laughing."

"Just so long as you die."

Deciding she'd had more than enough, Buffy darted forward. Percy put his head down and rushed. Buffy gave a grunt as the vampire's crew-cut head rammed into the pit of her stomach. With a roar, Percy kept on going, slamming Buffy up hard against the nearest wall. Buffy's head whipped back, hitting the bricks with a sickening smack. Her whole head roared with pain. Bright pinpoints of hot, white light danced at the edges of her eyes.

Automatically, she locked her knees to keep herself steady, keep her body from sliding down the wall. She shook her head, desperately trying to clear her vision. There were two Percys now.

"I just love that sound, don't you?" they said as they danced backward, out of staking range. Smart vamps would have pressed their advantage, but not the Percys. They were too into the cat-and-mouse thing.

"The last one's head sounded like that too," the Percys confided. "Just like a nice ripe watermelon. Don't worry, though. She didn't feel a thing. Not by that time."

Buffy managed to suck in a breath, the first since her close encounter with the vampire's cranium. Her head felt like it was being worked on by a burly construction worker with an enormous jackhammer.

She shook her head again, harder this time. Nerve endings screamed in protest. A burst of colored lights joined the white ones at the edges of her eyes. But it worked. Her vision cleared. No concussion. *Excellent.*

Now there was just one incredibly annoying vampire standing in front of her. One incredibly annoying vampire who didn't have very long to live, if Buffy Summers had anything to say about it.

"Don't you ever lose the urge to talk?"

"Well, you wanted to know about the others," Percy protested in a hurt voice. "If you don't want to know, you shouldn't ask. You don't have to go and be all rude about it."

"Is that what Mama says?" Buffy asked. She sidled

toward him. Closing. She was halfway across the alley when her progress was halted by a wailing cry.

"Maamaa . . ."

To Buffy's astonishment, Webster reappeared at the entrance to the alley with Angel right behind him.

"How come you're back?" the Slayer asked.

"I think it's a twin bonding thing," Angel answered as he and Webster hurtled toward her.

"Webster, look out!" Percy shouted. But it was already too late. Buffy stuck her foot out. Webster went flying, his navy blue tie streaming out over his shoulder. He landed in the row of trash cans opposite the back door of the Bronze and lay still. With a snarl of rage, Percy leaped for Angel's back.

Angel spun around, then backed up full force. This time, it was Percy's head that made that lovely watermelon sound. Once, twice, Angel hurled himself back against the side of the Bronze. But Percy continued to cling like a leech.

"Back-up plan," Buffy called out. Angel staggered forward. Buffy ran straight at the wall, took two quick banking steps up it. Then she flipped, twisting in midair and came straight down, stake plunging. Straight into the middle of Percy's unprotected back.

Snarling in pain and rage, he threw his head back. His feral yellow eyes focused on Buffy for a fraction of a second.

"Mama isn't going to like this one little bit," he said.

Buffy pulled the stake out and Percy crumbled.

"Let's hope she knows how to use a Dust-Buster."

Angel brushed vamp dust off his shoulders.

"Oh, sorry," Buffy said, reaching up to help.

Angel shrugged. "No problem."

Together, Buffy and Angel turned to where Webster lay in a heap of overturned trash cans at the back of the alley. Buffy seriously hoped that none of the Bronze's rowdier patrons had deposited anything too disgusting in them lately. She had a feeling Webster the whiner wasn't coming out. That meant she'd have to go in after him.

"You killed my brother," Webster complained. He sat up with a rustle of garbage. "You weren't supposed to do that."

"Says who?" Buffy asked. *The Young Vampire Book of Etiquette and Good Living?*

"I think you mean dying," Angel said.

"I don't like you," Webster told him.

"Well, that certainly ruins my night."

"Don't worry," Buffy consoled Angel. "I won't let him hurt your feelings. I'll take care of him for you."

"Mama!" Webster screamed. "Mama, help me! Where are you?"

"Webster!" Buffy heard a far-off voice bellow.

Instantly, Angel spun around, placing himself so he was back-to-back with Buffy. "I vote we wrap this round up," he said. "Sounds like the cavalry's coming."

"Don't you just hate parental interference?" Buffy muttered.

Webster rose from the nest of tumbled trash cans like a phoenix from the ashes. He had a Snickers bar wrapper stuck to the front of his shirt. Buffy figured that was appropriate.

"You can't kill me," Webster taunted. "Not now that my Mama's coming. She'll protect me, you'll see. And she'll make you sorry for what you did to Percy."

"Webster! Percy!" a voice from the mouth of the alley cried. "Boys, where are you? You know how I feel about you sneaking off behind my back. It's not nice to tease your mama."

At her own back, Buffy felt Angel abruptly tense. "Don't turn around," he cautioned.

"Why not?"

"Because I don't think you're going to like it."

"I'm here, Mama!" Webster yelped. He took a few faltering steps away from the garbage and pointed a trembling finger at Buffy. "She *killed* Percy, Mama! She stabbed him in the back. She didn't even let him die with honor."

Buffy heard the mother vampire growl low in her throat, and felt her stomach twist at the sound. She didn't have to turn around. She'd heard that sound before. Enough times to know what evil sounded like, and that it always sounded the same, no matter what it looked like.

"Brazen hussy," the mother vampire's voice snaked through the alley to wrap around Buffy. "Coward."

"Well, make up your mind," Buffy called back. "Which is it?"

Her only answer was the sound of high-heeled shoes moving inexorably down the alley.

"Get away from my boy," the vampire mother hissed. "If you do, I promise to go easy on you. I'll only kill you."

"I told you so," Webster taunted, his tone triumphant. "My mama's here now. You can't—"

Without warning, the back door of the Bronze opened and a figure stumbled into the alley. One who had consumed a little more libation than could be considered good for him, it might be said. One hand was clapped across his mouth, the other across his stomach.

"Get back!" Buffy shouted.

Startled, the figure lifted its head. In the fitful light of the alley, Buffy saw his bleary eyes focus not on her, but on something over her shoulder. Saw his eyes go wide, wider, widest—his face turn the color of milk.

He whirled around, doubling over. And lost his evening's worth of bar snack food.

"Eeewww!" Webster cried out. "Look what you've done to my new shoes!"

Okay, Buffy thought, *that's it. Time to wrap things up and get out of here.*

She took two quick steps, shoved overindulgence boy back inside the Bronze and slammed the door behind him with a swift kick.

Behind her, she heard the vampire mother roar into action. Heard the heavy sound of bone against bone as she and Angel slammed together, then parted. The mother vampire growled again, the sound wild and feral. Buffy raised the stake that was still held tight in her fist, and took one more step forward.

"My mama's right behind you," Webster warned nervously, trying to back up a step. His feet skidded on the new substance on the floor of the alley. "You can't—"

This time, it was Buffy who cut him off. She took one final step, her foot sliding as her arm flashed out in a short, swift jab. The stake caught Webster, square in the chest.

"You wanna bet?" the Slayer asked.

"Hey!" Webster said. "You did it anyway. That's no fair! You weren't supposed to do that." Then, like his brother, he crumbled into dust. The Snickers wrapper hovered in the air, then dropped back down to lie among the rest of the refuse.

Buffy heard the alley go absolutely still behind her.

Slowly, she turned around, then froze. Now, she, too could see the vampire mother, standing just beyond Angel about halfway down the alley.

She was tall, almost as tall as Angel was, and she was definitely a whole lot wider. She was wearing a dress of turquoise blue, splattered with enormous white flowers. They looked like daisies but it was hard for Buffy to be sure. They were so large. And there were so many of them.

She could see that the centers of the flowers were the same color as the vampire mother's eyes, though. A fierce and blazing yellow.

Her hair was piled in a great twisting mass on top of her head, held in place by a huge clip studded with rhinestones. Her feet were encased in turquoise shoes with daisy buckles on them.

Buffy could feel the tension whipping through the air, so thick she could have sworn it had substance, form, its own body. And there was something else as well. Something that would have loved to tear her limb from limb right where she stood.

Hatred. Pure. Simple. Potent.

Angel's right, Buffy thought. *I don't like this. Not at all.*

Into the charged silence, Angel spoke.

"I have a bad feeling about this."

Buffy opened her mouth to answer, but she never got the chance. The vampire mother threw back her head and opened her jaws. A wild keening filled the air of the alley.

Angel staggered back and pulled Buffy against him as if to offer shelter as the cry roared around them, cold and biting as a winter wind. Seeking. Scourging. Longing for their destruction.

Buffy'd known evil had a sound, a voice, and so did grief. But she'd never known the two could speak with the same tongue until that moment.

On, on, on, the cry wailed, until it was Buffy's entire world, her entire universe. All she knew, all she'd ever known. All that she'd be able to remember. It would echo throughout the ages, the sound of this cry. It would still be going on when Hell froze over.

For all she knew, it would even cause it.

Buffy wanted to clap her hands over her ears, but forced herself to remain still. If she gave in to her impulse to do whatever it took to block out that sound, the vampire mother would have an advantage over her, she was sure of it.

From somewhere deep inside, she summoned up a single thought.

And the "Jeopardy" question is, *what is bloodcurdling?*

Then, as abruptly as it had begun, the cry ended. Once more, there fell a silence. So pure and complete, Buffy could hear the rush of blood through her veins. The expansion and contraction of her breath. Her heart, desperately pounding.

I am alive, she thought. *I am human.* The creature before her might be able to produce a cry wild and fierce enough to wake the dead. But then it only made sense. She *was* one.

Then Buffy saw the mother vampire take one step forward.

"Uh oh," Angel said from his position beside her.

"No kidding," Buffy answered. "Do you see the size of the flowers on that dress?"

"You killed my boys," the mother vamp hissed through her jagged teeth. "And now I'm going to make you pay for it."

Joyce Summers sat in her living room, pictures of her daughter spread out around her.

Buffy's earliest years were already in the scrapbook. Her infancy. Her toddler years. Kindergarten graduation. The beginnings of the progression of grade-school pictures.

Joyce had put in the photograph of Buffy sitting in her first red wagon in the driveway of their house in Los Angeles, her father, with his hand on the handle of the wagon, kneeling down beside her.

And then there was the one of her sitting naked in the bathtub, surrounded by mounds of ethereal white bubbles and holding out her rubber ducky like she'd just won the Oscar.

There was an early birthday party, with a cake that contained a real doll. The cake itself was the doll's skirt. It had taken her an entire morning to do the ruffle icing decorations, Joyce remembered. And Buffy and her friends about five minutes to demolish the whole thing.

Buffy still had the doll.

It had been one of the things she'd insisted on packing herself when they'd moved from LA to Sunnydale, along with her stuffed pig, Mr. Gordo.

Joyce flipped to the next blank page, pulled the clear, sticky film back and stared at the photographs on the coffee table in front of her. After a moment's consideration, she selected a picture of Buffy and her favorite cousin, Celia. It was one of the few pictures she had of the two girls together. Celia had died when she was eight years old.

The two girls stood together with their arms around each other. Celia was wearing jeans and a tee shirt. Normal kid clothes. But Buffy was wearing her Power Girl costume. She'd been so into being Power Girl she never wanted to take the costume off.

The only way I could wash it was by taking it off her while she slept, Joyce recalled.

She slid the photo onto the page and swiftly selected another, one of Buffy and her father standing side by side. Buffy was wearing a frilly pink party dress, tights, white patent-leather shoes with a matching purse. Her lips were curved up in honor of the camera, but the smile didn't reach her eyes.

This was Buffy's eighth birthday, when she hadn't wanted a party because Celia couldn't be there. Celia wasn't ever coming to one of Buffy's parties again. She was dead; she was gone. As a special treat, to try to cheer her up, Buffy's father had taken her to the ice show for the very first time.

Below the birthday picture Joyce placed one other from several months later. Buffy holding her own pair of ice skates. Her eyes still had shadows in them, but this time, they smiled.

Joyce slid the photo into the scrapbook, smoothed the sticky film over it, her own eyes suddenly blind.

How did it happen? she wondered.

How had her daughter grown up so fast? Grown up to be something neither of them could have predicted, perhaps even something neither of them wanted. Joyce understood that what Buffy was, what she did, was terribly important. Something literally no one else could be or do.

But choosing was not the same as being chosen.

And whatever Buffy might have chosen had been lost along the way. She was the Chosen One, the Slayer. Everything else was secondary. And the fact that her mother might grieve in moments for all the things Buffy would never have the chance to be didn't change a thing. What Joyce wanted, what Buffy might have chosen, could no longer be considered relevant.

Abruptly, Joyce slid the scrapbook off her lap and padded into the kitchen. She opened the freezer. Just as she thought. Buffy'd finished the ice cream and forgotten to say anything about it. If Joyce wanted some, she'd have to do a quick run to the store.

But suddenly, she longed for something sweet. Something cold. Anything that would drive this hot, dry ache from the back of her throat. She loved her daughter. Was working hard to honor what she was. But there were times, quiet nights like this, when the work was very, very hard.

Purposefully now, Joyce strode back into the living room, kicked off her slippers, and yanked her sneakers on. She wasn't going to sit around brooding about things that couldn't be changed or helped. She was made of sterner stuff than that, same as her daughter.

Besides, the scrapbook was supposed to be a celebration of Buffy, wasn't it? Of course it was.

But still, one hand on the door, the other holding tightly to the strap of her purse, Joyce Summers, the mother of the Slayer, paused. And uttered the same prayer a thousand mothers, a million, uttered on a million different nights, in every language a mind could think of. Though none prayed more fervently than Joyce did, or with such cause.

Please, she thought. *Just let my child be safe.*

Whatever she was doing. Wherever she was.

CHAPTER 6

"Any suggestions?" Buffy asked.

"Sorry," Angel said. "Fresh out."

"We could flip a coin," Buffy suggested. "Heads, we fight. Tails, we fight."

"Okay, we fight."

"I just knew you'd say that."

The mother vampire raised her arms, exposing half an inch of lacy, white slip and a sneaking suspicion of the top of panty hose. Buffy was unable to resist a shudder.

She'd had to fight things that turned her stomach before, but she hadn't figured they'd include somebody's mom. And definitely not a mom dressed in a glow-in-the-dark turquoise blue dress adorned by daisies the size of dinner plates. And who accessorized with rhinestones.

She guessed it was true, what they said. Whoever

"they" were. There really was a first time for everything.

Feet planted, Buffy and Angel stood side by side, their backs to the back door of the Bronze. Buffy could feel the adrenaline pumping through her veins.

"I get to count this time."

But before she could start, the mother vampire threw back her head and gave another great undulating wail. Fisting her hands in her hair, she pulled it down around her shoulders to lie in a seething mass, tangled and wild. She scraped her nails down her cheeks. Tore at her clothes.

Then, step by step, she began to move toward Buffy and Angel. Instantly, by mutual, silent accord, they took a step apart. It was harder to fight two moving targets than one. Buffy didn't even have to be the Slayer to figure that one out.

The mother vampire laughed low in her throat.

"You think I'm going to fight you, don't you?" she asked, her voice filled with scorn. "You think I'm going to waste the chance to avenge my sons' deaths by trying to deal with you myself."

The vampire mother halted her advance, her face wreathed in a horrible smile.

"Okay, now *I* have a bad feeling about this," Buffy said.

"You should, girl," said the vampire mother. "I'm going to make you wish you'd never been born."

Once more, the mother vampire threw back her head.

"Vengeance," she shouted, her voice harsh, distorted. "Powers of the Underworld, Powers of Darkness, hear my call. Hear the cry of a mother, begging for retribution. Answer my plea! Give me justice! Rise up and avenge the deaths of my sons!"

Above their heads, as if in answer, from a clear night sky, rolled one clap of thunder.

"I really hate it when they call for reinforcements," Angel said.

"I say we finish this now, before anything else shows up," Buffy said.

"I'm definitely with you on that."

Buffy took a gliding step forward. The mother vampire lowered her head and looked straight at her.

"Get ready," she said. "Your doom is coming."

"I think you mean it's at hand," Buffy said. "Only you've got it backward. *Your* doom. *My* hand."

She hefted the stake just as a blast of icy wind swept through the alley. So strong it stopped her in her tracks, then pushed her back. Buffy threw up her hands to protect her eyes from the biting, scouring air. She thought she could hear Angel shouting her name, but she couldn't be sure. The wind had its own voices.

Then, as quickly as it had come, the sudden gust was over. The air around Buffy grew perfectly still, absolutely quiet. Then, it began to shimmer with heat, as if the pavement of the alley was resting on some enormous stove top. Fine tendrils of mist began to rise. Red mist, dark as heart's blood. A mist the color of brimstone.

Hellfire.

"Why do I have the feeling this just isn't my night?" Buffy muttered.

Something exploded out of the air before her.

A woman. Towering. Majestic. Enormous. So tall she dwarfed all the other inhabitants of the alley, including the vampire mother. And that was saying something.

Atop the huge column that was her neck, four faces stared outward. Or at least Buffy assumed that there were four. She could only actually see three, the one staring straight at her, and the two glaring at the alley walls. But if ever anything was going to have eyes in the back of its head, Buffy figured this was it.

From nearby, Angel spoke. "I'd take a wild guess and say that's why."

"You win what's behind door number three," Buffy said. "Um—I don't suppose that's anyone you know?"

"Sorry," Angel said. "Not from my neighborhood."

The woman's skin was a strange, flat gray, a color Buffy had seen only once before. In pictures of what the Oregon countryside had looked like after the eruption of Mount St. Helens.

A color that wasn't a color. That was alive, yet denied life. In the barren landscape of that ashen face— those ashen faces—four pairs of red eyes glowed.

"I am Nemesis," the figure spoke out all four mouths at once. The tones diverged, then slid together, weaving around and through one another. Unified, then discordant, then unified once more. As if each voice told a slightly different version of the same story. Buffy felt their power resonating in the marrow of her bones.

"Nemesis," the figure repeated, "called the Balancer. Why have I been summoned?"

"To right a great wrong," the vampire mother shouted hoarsely. She strode forward to the side of Nemesis which faced Buffy. She threw herself at the giant figure's feet. "My beautiful boys, my babies, have been murdered, cut down. I call upon the Powers of Darkness to help me avenge their deaths."

"I have a better idea," Buffy said. "How about if you just join them?"

She took a step forward. Before she could take another, Nemesis raised a hand. The icy wind returned to sweep the alley. Buffy could feel it cut through her like knives. She faltered back a step, and the wind ceased.

"Okay," she panted. "I get it. No staking at the present time. But is it too much to ask for a little reality check?"

She pointed at the kneeling woman in the turquoise dress. "She is a vampire. Her beautiful baby boys were vampires. That makes them the bad guys. I'm the Slayer. I hunt vamps and wipe them out. That makes me the good guy."

"So you say," Nemesis replied. Buffy watched the red eyes facing her flick to Angel, then flick back. "Yet I see you also hunt *with* a vampire."

How does she know that? Buffy wondered. Angel was no longer in vamp mode. Though, technically, Buffy supposed Angel still qualified as a card-carrying member of the Powers of Darkness. Apparently, it took one to know one.

"He's different," she said, the urge to protect Angel punching straight from the center of her gut. Atavistic. Primal. The age-old instinct to safeguard one's mate. Buffy'd long since stopped questioning it. It was what it was.

The fire in Nemesis's eyes blazed out with what Buffy swore was amusement as the red orbs looked Angel up and down.

"I can see that he is different," Nemesis said at last. "So this is the Cursed One."

"I hate being recognized in public," Angel said. "What'd I do, make the front page of the *Underworld Inquirer?*"

Nemesis shrugged. "Word gets around. It's a small Underworld, after all. Though I admit I've always taken a personal interest in your case. In deciding to curse you rather than try to kill you, the Gypsies displayed such a fine sense of proportion. Tell me, do you enjoy being what you are and having a soul?"

"You're the Balancer, you figure it out," Angel said shortly.

"I really hate to interrupt," Buffy broke in, "but do you think we might have an on-task sort of moment?"

"Sorry," Angel muttered.

"So we're all agreed, right?" Buffy asked Nemesis. "Vampire Slayer, good. Vampire, bad. Vengeance, totally unnecessary. Out of the question. So you back off. I stake Mama and we all go home in time for the 'Late Show.' "

"No!" the vampire mother cried, scrambling to her feet. "I demand—"

"Silence!" Nemesis roared out. The mother vampire shut her mouth with a gnash of fangs. "You have called me. I have come. You will make no more demands. I will decide what must be done."

"But—" Buffy began.

A second blast of icy air shot through the alley.

"Silence!" Nemesis roared once more. "Do you think things are so simple, foolish mortal?"

Had other, earlier, Slayers had to contend with these kinds of spontaneous pop quizzes? Buffy wondered. Or was it just a modern-day type thing?

Note to self: Query Giles.

"That's a trick question, isn't it?" she asked.

Nemesis smiled.

"This creature has asked for vengeance, for retribution," she said, pointing to the vampire mother. "She called upon the Powers of Darkness, of the Underworld, to aid her, and I am what she summoned. Do you expect me to side with you?"

"She's got a point," Angel advised.

"I just knew you were going to say that," Buffy muttered.

"Listen up," Nemesis said. "Hear well what Nemesis has decided."

She pointed at the Slayer.

"You must undergo a trial. If you prevail, no harm will befall you. You will have proved your actions were just, that Balance has been served. The call for vengeance will be denied. But if you fail—"

"If she fails," the vampire mother spoke with relish. She turned her yellow eyes on Buffy. "If she fails, then Slayer or not, she is mine."

"You agree to the terms?" Nemesis asked.

"I agree," answered the mother vampire.

Nemesis clapped her hands together. "The pact is made," she declared.

"Wait a minute," Buffy protested. "Don't I get some say in this?"

"Think about it," Nemesis said. "You're the one on trial."

"Think again," Buffy shot back. "I'm not going through with your stupid trial."

"Somehow, I just knew you were going to feel that way," Nemesis answered. "Did I mention our trial offer has special incentives? Allow me introduce you to one."

She clapped her hands once more. There was a flash of hot, red light, so dazzling Buffy threw her hands up to shield her eyes.

When her vision cleared, Joyce was standing in the alley.

"Mom?"

Joyce Summers looked dazed, disoriented. As if anyone could blame her. She was dressed in the same pair of sweats she'd been wearing when Buffy'd left her earlier that evening. Left her safe. At home.

Joyce blinked rapidly, as if she couldn't quite see her surroundings. She had her purse, Buffy noticed. As if she'd decided to make a late night run to the store.

Ice cream, probably, Buffy thought with a quick pang of conscience. She'd finished the last of it herself and hadn't put it on the list.

Then she noticed the way her mother was holding the purse, clutched to her chest like a life preserver.

Buffy felt something rise within her. The double whammy. Rage and terror. She struggled to keep them under control. If ever there was a time to keep her head, this was it.

The Powers of Darkness have taken my mom.

"Buffy, honey, is that you?" Joyce said, her voice quavering just a little as she peered in the direction of the sound of Buffy's voice. "Sweetheart, what's going on?"

"I think we're all agreed now, aren't we?" Nemesis said. "We will proceed with the trial."

She clapped her hands a third time and Joyce disappeared.

"Wait!" Buffy cried desperately. "Where are you taking her? What have you done with my mom?"

"Assuming you make it through the trial then you'll know," Nemesis said. "You have one hour in which to prepare. Bring no weapons."

Her red eyes flicked briefly over Angel. "Come alone. Name the place of the trial," Nemesis instructed the vampire mother.

The mother vampire stepped forward and extended one hand toward Buffy. In it was an elaborately decorated calling card.

Buffy took the card. Read the address.

"Two thousand Elysian Fields Lane? You must be joking."

In answer, the vampire mother simply grinned. "It does have a certain ring to it under the circumstances, doesn't it? Be prompt, Slayer. You're going to fail. I'm going to be there to pick up the pieces."

"Enough!" Nemesis proclaimed.

She clapped her hands a fourth time. Thick red mist engulfed the alley. When it cleared, Buffy and Angel were alone.

"We don't have much time," Angel said at once. "We should get going."

Buffy stood frozen, as if rooted to the spot. Angel moved to her, put a hand on her shoulder.

"Buffy?"

As if his touch had somehow freed her from a spell, Buffy started, then sprang into action.

"You can't come with me, Angel," she said, as she sprinted toward the mouth of the alley. "You heard what that four-faced whatever-it-was said. I have to go alone."

Angel made a dash to keep up, brought Buffy to a halt by seizing her by one arm.

"You're can't go anywhere until we know more about what you're dealing with," he said urgently. "We should go find Giles."

Buffy shook his arm off, wishing she could as easily shake off the need to scream, to weep.

The Powers of Darkness have taken my mom.

And they had no right to, no right at all. Not that a little detail like that had ever stopped them, of course.

"I don't have time for Giles. I may have to play this stupid game, but I don't see why I have to abide by anyone's rules but my own. I'm not going to wait an hour, Angel. I'm going to go *right now.* Maybe I can take them by surprise if I do."

She didn't want to wait. Couldn't wait.

The Powers of Darkness have taken my mom.

Angel gave her a shake, grasping both her shoulders tightly.

"I understand what you're feeling," he said. "I know how much you want to save your mom. But you heard what Nemesis said, Buffy. You can't take any weapons with you. Knowledge may be the only one you've got. If you go without it, you truly go unarmed."

Buffy opened her mouth to lash out at him. To deny

the sense of what he was saying. How could Angel understand her need to rescue her mother? He'd murdered his own.

In the next instant shame swept through her, hot and potent. What had Nemesis asked him? *How does it feel to be what you are* and *have a soul?*

Like nothing I can imagine, Buffy thought. But it was how she knew he was right, and she was wrong. If there was anyone who understood the pain, and the value, of knowing what you faced, it was Angel.

Just for an instant, Buffy leaned forward to let her head rest against his chest. If he'd been human, she'd have heard his beating heart.

She felt Angel's fingers stroke briefly through her hair.

"The clock's running," he whispered. "Let's go."

CHAPTER 7

Alone, in the white house on the hill, the vampire mother paced the portrait gallery, grieving for the loss of her beloved baby boys.

Naturally, she'd taken time to change her clothes.

Hair once more upswept, this time beneath a black pillbox hat. Body covered by a simple black dress. Against her ample bosom, a single string of milk-white pearls glowed. Low-heeled black pumps. Black gloves that fastened at the wrist with a single pearl button. A spray of long-stemmed blood-red roses in her arms.

It was important to keep up appearances, even in a time of sorrow.

A true lady never lost control, never gave way to her emotions. Her sons' murderer had already caused the vampire mother to lose control once, in a way that, under normal circumstances, she would have considered most unbecoming.

83

Still, she couldn't entirely regret her outburst. It had brought her Nemesis, after all. Nemesis, the Balancer, the bringer of retribution. The one who would avenge the deaths of her sons.

Unless the unthinkable actually happens and the murdering tramp survives the trial.

The vampire mother shuddered as she traversed the length of the gallery, her heels clicking against the cold white marble, until she finally came to a halt before the full-length portrait of her husband. He stared down upon her, stern and proud. But, for the first time in more than a hundred years, she could hardly bring herself to look back.

She had failed him. Failed herself. Failed in her duty. She had not protected their sons.

With a strangled cry, the vampire mother fell to her knees before the portrait of her long-dead husband. Her fingers clawed the blossoms she held in her arms. Scattering a shower of petals across the marble, surrounding herself in a sea of red rose blood.

And there, on her knees, she embraced her new duty. Made a new vow.

"I swear to you that our sons will be avenged," she promised, her voice choked and harsh. "I will make their murderer pay for what she has done. Here, in this house, she will undergo her trial."

Nemesis would bring the murderer to her. She had made certain of that. Just as she would make certain of something else.

"Win the trial, or lose, it will make no difference," the vampire mother promised her long-dead husband, at long last looking up into his eyes.

"Once the murderer of our sons crosses this threshold, I will make certain she never leaves. Alive."

"Come on, Giles. I don't have much time."

Buffy paced the Sunnydale High library. She'd been unable to sit still since she'd arrived. Angel had taken off to patrol and check a few sources for more info on the Mama Vamp.

Buffy had found Giles at his desk, working late, a thing she'd earlier counted on. Giles never seemed to tire of spending time with his books.

And if that wasn't a big red flag signaling that her Watcher needed to get a life, Buffy didn't know what was. She appreciated books. Books were good, in their proper time and place. Which, for her, definitely didn't include Saturday night.

Still, she had to admit Giles's dedication to all tomes dark and musty, all reference papers great and small, did come in handy on occasion.

Like say, for instance, now.

"Just give me another moment," Giles answered, marking a place in the book before him. He looked up, taking his glasses off and using one tweed-clad forearm to wipe his brow.

"Buffy," he said, his tone betraying the combination of compassion and annoyance that Buffy had come to associate with him, "I do wish you'd sit down. You're wasting your energy prowling about like that."

"Yeah," Xander said. "Not to mention making those unsightly trenches in the floor."

At least there's one thing going my way in all this, Buffy thought, as she plunked down with a sigh. The gang had already arranged to meet at the library ahead of time. That meant Buffy hadn't had to waste valuable moments tracking them down.

Moments being things in rather short supply.

They'd arrived shortly after Buffy herself had. A quick check-in had confirmed the gang had completed their mission: Suz Tompkins had been safely delivered to her door.

Buffy supposed she'd accomplished her mission, too. She'd taken care of the guys who'd been after Suz, and who'd been responsible for the disappearances of Leila and Heidi. It was just her bad luck she wasn't going to get the chance to rest on her laurels.

She listened to the sound of pages turning from opposite ends of the library. Willow and Giles. As usual, Giles had put the gang to work as soon as he'd known there was a problem. Willow was assigned the task of looking up references to Nemesis, while Giles himself tried to uncover more information about the vampire mother and her boys.

Oz was helping Willow; he'd toted the books she'd asked for to her table and arranged them into two huge piles. Xander had an assignment, too—to stay out of the way and not interrupt.

Buffy hadn't gotten a clear look at the volume Giles was so engrossed in, but she was pretty sure it had a mouthful of a title like, *American Vampires of the Nineteenth Century: An Historical Retrospective and Chronology.*

Giles's theory was that determining who the vamps Buffy'd dusted were might provide a key to what she might confront in her upcoming trial. As usual, Giles was leaving no stone unturned. Buffy appreciated his thoroughness. She really did. She just wished he'd get those stones rolling, preferably, sometime soon.

She pulled the scrunchie from her hair and rotated her neck to relieve some of the tension she felt building, using the action to sneak a glance at the library clock. 11:23 P.M. Not quite half an hour after she'd been informed she'd have to undergo a trial to rescue her mother.

It felt like a lifetime.

Buffy began to tap her foot, trying not to think of the way Joyce had looked in the alley behind the Bronze. Clutching her purse to her chest as if it could protect her.

Frightened. Lost. Alone.

Buffy knew what it was to feel like that. She didn't want her mom to know. One Summers in the family facing seemingly insurmountable odds was more than enough.

"Here we are," Giles said suddenly. "I think I've got it now, though it's rather incomplete, I'm sorry to say. There are gaps in the record, but, then, there almost always are."

Buffy bit the inside of her cheek to master her impatience. "Just tell me what you've got, Giles."

"What I have is a reference to an entire family of Confederates being sired," Giles explained, hefting the reference book he'd chosen. "According to this, it happened in 1864, toward the end of the Civil War. During the fall of Atlanta, or shortly thereafter, apparently. The name of the family was Walker."

"Wait, wait, don't tell me," Xander broke in. "Was there a guy named Rhett Butler involved?"

Giles set the book down with a *thump*.

"While under ordinary circumstances I would choose this moment to applaud the fact that you have actually made a literary reference, Xander, I—"

"What literary reference?" Xander interrupted, obviously startled. "I'm talking about a movie—you know—*Gone With the Wind?*"

"Xander," Willow spoke up for the first time. "Remember first grade? The library is supposed to be quiet time."

"Yes, well, as I was saying," Giles went on. "It appears that Mr. Walker was an officer in the Confederate army. How he became a vampire, who was responsible for it, isn't really specified. What is known is that he deserted and returned to his family during the siege of Atlanta. He changed his wife. She then changed their two fifteen-year-old sons. The entire family escaped as the city of Atlanta was burning."

"Talk about family values," Oz put in.

Giles's eyebrows rose. "Quite," he replied. "The father was, er, dispatched several years later, leaving just the mother and the two sons. They're identical twins, by the way. Did I mention that?"

"In that case," Buffy said, "they're definitely our boys. Anything else?"

Giles took his glasses off and rubbed the bridge of his nose. "Regretfully, no. This is really only a chronology, not an in-depth study of nineteenth-century American vampires."

"Who writes books like that?" Xander wondered aloud.

"Trust me," Giles responded. "You don't want to know."

"It doesn't really help me anyway, does it?" Buffy interrupted. "Aside from the information about how they were sired, it isn't anything we don't already know. Including the fact that Vamp Mama suffers from a pretty major case of attachment disorder."

She switched her attention to Willow, turning around in her chair to look at her. "Anything on Nemesis, Will?"

A worried expression crossed the redhead's face. She gestured to the two stacks of books beside her.

"I'm not so sure," she acknowledged. "There's the dictionary definition, and the historical definition. Which do you want first?"

"All of those are dictionaries?" Xander said. "The mind boggles. Okay, okay, I remember," he said, holding up his hands like he was being taken hostage as Willow glanced over at him. "I'll be as quiet as a little library mouse from now on."

"Go with the dictionary, Will," Buffy said.

Willow opened the largest of the volumes. The print was so small, it took a magnifying glass to read it.

"Nemesis," Willow read aloud. "An agent or act of retribution; someone or something that defeats or destroys one; an opponent whom one cannot best."

"Nice," Buffy said. "I'm thinking ignorance just might have been bliss on that one."

"Well," Willow said, her tone encouraging. "Then there's the historical stuff. They almost all say the same thing. Nemesis was originally a Greek deity. A goddess."

That thing I saw in the alley was a goddess? Buffy thought.

"Of what?"

"Retribution," Willow answered. "Also, evil deeds, as in avenger of."

"Well, everything should be okay, then." Oz spoke

up from his place beside her. "Buffy did what she was supposed to do. Dusted vamps. Not exactly my definition of an evil deed."

"I tried that line of reasoning," Buffy said. "I didn't get very far. The vampire mother called upon the Powers of Darkness, and this Nemesis thing answered the call. I'd say it doesn't look real good for our definition of evil deeds."

"But that doesn't make any sense," Willow protested.

"Well, actually—" Giles began.

"I knew there was going to be a catch," Xander muttered.

Buffy shot to her feet. Enough of this sitting still thing. It was getting her nowhere, and the clock was ticking. Less than half an hour to go to the trial now.

"Actually, what?" she asked.

"Well, logically speaking," Giles said, "there's only a discrepancy if you try to place Nemesis within our own framework of right and wrong. But if you place her outside that framework—"

"Or inside the framework of the Powers of Darkness—" Willow broke in.

"Exactly," Giles nodded. "Viewed that way, there's no discrepancy at all. In fact, it makes perfect sense, if viewed in that light. The Slayer would be the one perpetrating an evil deed, to an agent of the Powers of Darkness. We may not agree with the perspective, but the reasoning does have its own internal integrity."

"Does he ever explain things in English?" Xander complained.

"I *am* English," Giles answered shortly.

"But, she called herself the Balancer," Willow said. "Shouldn't that help our side?"

Giles slid his glasses back into place. "It should, but I'm far from certain that it's going to," he replied.

"In fact, I think it's safe to assume that Buffy herself has already raised the salient point. Nemesis was *summoned* by the vampire mother. Whatever Nemesis's original purpose may have been, she is now an agent of the Powers of Darkness. The safest course is to assume the trial she's set up may not be fair and may be very unpleasant."

"Great," the Slayer muttered.

"Well, then, we'll just make it more fair. You know—even the playing field," Willow said hotly. She got up from her chair and moved to Buffy. "We won't let you go alone. We never let you go alone, if we can help it. Now is not a good time to start. Not a good day to start new things. I read that in my horoscope."

Buffy put a hand on her friend's shoulder. "I have to go alone, Will," she said softly. "That four-faced thing has got my mom. I'm going to do whatever it takes to get her back. That means following her rules: going alone and unarmed. I've done it before. I can do it again."

"But—" Willow said.

"No buts," the Slayer answered. "This has to be my fight, Will. My fight alone. If you really want to help me, you'll stay safe."

And out of my way.

"Well, okay," Willow finally gave in. "But I don't have to like it."

"We'll keep researching," Giles promised. "Maybe we can come up with something more."

"Fine," Buffy nodded. A strained silence fell across the library. Nobody asked how they were going to get the something more to her once they'd found it.

"And stay focused," Giles spoke up just before Buffy reached the door. "Don't let yourself be distracted by potential tricks Nemesis might offer. Get to the trial. Get your mother. Get out."

"Got it," said Buffy.

"And keep your wits about you."

"I was pretty much planning on taking them along." *As they're about the only things I can take*, the Slayer added silently.

"And—"

"Giles," Buffy said, as she pulled the library door open.

"Yes?"

"I'm going."

"Yes, well—good luck," he said.

"Thanks," Buffy answered. She released the door, heard it *click* closed behind her. Shutting out her friends, her Watcher.

I'm on my own now, Buffy thought. Not even Angel, who could often go where the others couldn't, could help her.

She was the only thing that stood between her mother and an uncertain fate.

Don't just stand there, get moving, she told herself.

Now, more than ever, every second counted.

Ten minutes later, Buffy was at home, moving through it with the single-minded determination of a heat-seeking missile. She rifled the contents of closets, pawed through drawers. No weapons, Nemesis had said.

But that isn't the same as going empty-handed, is it?

The trouble was, with Nemesis making all the rules, it was awfully hard for Buffy to know what qualified as a weapon and what didn't. And she didn't want to weigh herself down with a bunch of miscellaneous stuff. There was no telling what she might be called upon to fight during the course of her upcoming trial.

Exasperated, she shut the door of the bathroom medicine cabinet with a *snap* of irritation. What did she think she was going to find in there? Did she think she could save her mother by brandishing her toothbrush?

Try as she might, Buffy just couldn't bring herself to believe that the fact that she brushed so hard the bristles all stuck out sideways was going to be all that terrifying to things that could be summoned by the Powers of Darkness.

She opened a drawer, snatched out a scrunchie to replace the one she'd forgotten at the library, yanked her hair back in a ponytail and secured it.

Streamlined is best, she thought, as she headed back to her bedroom to change her clothes. Fewer things for the whatever-they-weres she was about to encounter to grab onto.

She smiled a little grimly as she realized she was giving herself the same advice she'd given Suz Tompkins at the mall. Never give your enemy a handhold.

Quickly, Buffy changed into a pair of tight black pants, pulled on a shirt, and slipped into her sturdiest pair of boots. The boots made her feel a little better. If she was going to kick the ass of the Powers of Darkness, she wanted to make as big an impression on it as she possibly could.

Her mother never liked it when she did the basic

black routine. But then, Buffy had to figure this was one time when even her mom would have to admit that what Buffy wore didn't make a difference.

She shivered, suddenly. The truth was, Buffy felt a little naked without something from her Slayer's bag of tricks. On impulse, she returned to her closet, pulled out the leather jacket Angel had given her a lifetime ago and slipped that on, too. The fact that it had pockets was somehow comforting.

Not that she had anything to put in them, of course.

She looked at the glowing numbers of the digital clock on her dresser. Ten minutes to midnight. Time to get going. Trying to ignore the way her heart was pounding like a bad bass line, she headed for the front door.

She got as far as the living room, then stopped dead.

There, on the couch, illuminated by a pool of light from a nearby lamp, lay her mother's scrapbook project. Exactly as Joyce had left it, looking for all the world as if she had simply stepped away of her own accord and would return to it at any moment.

Buffy felt her racing heart shudder, her breath clog in her lungs.

Her mother hadn't stepped away of her own free will. She'd been snatched by the Powers of Darkness. Taken from her home because of something Buffy had done. A thing she'd had to do. Because she was the Slayer. She was the Chosen One.

Because of Buffy, her mother was in danger. It wasn't the first time, and it might not be the last. Neither of which made Buffy feel even one bit better.

She knew time was of the essence, could practically hear the minutes till the trial would begin ticking by inside her head. But still, her feet carried her to the couch, her eyes glued to the scrapbook her mother was creating as a tribute to her. The one designed to celebrate Buffy, honor her passage from child to adulthood.

Buffy looked down at the page on top, the one her mother had been working on when she'd been so rudely interrupted. Several photos were already inside the clear, sticky film. One more sat on top as if just waiting to be added. Buffy stooped and picked it up.

A picture of herself at about age ten looked back at her. The young Buffy was cocky, full of life. Grinning straight into the eye of the camera.

I remember that day, Buffy thought. The whole family had gone to a park, and her dad had pushed her on a swing, higher than she'd ever gone before, until the young girl she'd been had shrieked with a sound that only came from the throats of children: terror and laughter inextricably mixed.

Going so high, high, high up in the sky had been terrifying and wonderful all at once. Because, in her heart, Buffy hadn't really been frightened at all. She'd known her parents were right there, beside her. With the certainty of childhood, she'd known what that meant: that nothing bad could really happen, no harm could truly befall her.

Buffy set the photo back down beside the ones already in the scrapbook. She remembered these, also. There she was with her cousin, Celia, who'd died too young. And there was Buffy on her eighth birthday, when her father had taken her to the ice show for the very first time.

A thing he didn't do anymore, no matter how much her heart might want him to. But then, she hadn't told her father what was in her heart for a very long time.

Because now, little Buffy Summers was all grown up. Her parents were divorced. Her father was far away. Now, he sent her a card with a check in it for her birthday. If he remembered. If she was lucky.

And her mom, who'd stuck by her no matter what, her mom was the one who was in harm's way. Because the child in that picture had grown up to be the Slayer, the Chosen One. A thing over which she'd had absolutely no choice.

And her mother hadn't either, Buffy realized suddenly.

She'd kept what she was from her mother for a long time. For a lot of reasons. Had this been one of them? Had Buffy instinctively known that, while Joyce might freak, she would never walk away? That she would cling to her daughter, claiming her for her own no matter what she was?

Buffy's friends had made a conscious choice to be part of her world as the Slayer. Sure, she would have been hurt if they'd decided to turn their backs on her and walk away. But she would have understood, been unable to blame them for it.

The world was a more comforting place, an easier place, if you didn't know what Buffy knew. If you didn't have to face the fact that it wasn't always a safe one.

Joyce Summers had never had a choice but to face facts. Joyce was bound to Buffy because of who Joyce was: nothing more nor less than the Slayer's mother.

Buffy moved to stand in the center of the living room, staring at her reflection in the mirror above the fireplace. Was that little girl, the one her mother was preserving so lovingly, still somewhere inside her?

Perhaps the whole purpose of the scrapbook was to remind her that it was. Perhaps her mother had understood more than Buffy had ever given her credit for or realized.

Understood what it felt like to have your past cast into doubt by a future you'd never asked for and couldn't control. A future which had revealed her to be the Chosen One.

And now her mother had been chosen, also. As an instrument of retribution, of revenge, a way to get back at Buffy. And there was only one thing Buffy could do about it. *Not screw up.* The scrapbook sitting behind her on the couch all but screamed aloud her mother's faith in her. Her mother's love.

Now it was Buffy's turn to prove her own. And to prove her mother's faith was justified.

She was just about to turn, filled with fresh determination, when her eyes caught sight of something resting on the mantel. The box of matches her mom always had ready, for lighting candles for special occasions.

A series of images exploded behind Buffy's eyes.

Her mother, lighting candles for Thanksgiving dinners, for birthdays, for no reason at all. No reason except she wanted to make something special for herself.

For me, Buffy thought.

She took two quick steps, snatched the box of matches from the mantel, and stuffed them into her jacket pocket. *Nemesis has forgotten something,* she thought.

Something that Buffy herself had almost forgotten. Something she might not have remembered, if not for her mom.

A Slayer didn't need to bring any weapons with her. Because a Slayer's best weapon was always herself.

CHAPTER 8

Who does Buffy Summers think she is? Suz Tompkins wondered.

Crouched in the bushes of the yard across the street, the camouflage jacket she'd chosen blending in with the shrubbery around her, Suz watched as Buffy left the house. Noted the way she moved down the sidewalk at a brisk walk, not rushing, but definitely not wasting any time.

In the glare of a streetlight, Suz could even see the expression on Buffy's face. Determined. Set.

She walks like she knows where she's going.

Well, as far as Suz was concerned, that was just fine. Because Buffy wasn't the only one who knew where she was going. Suz knew, too.

She was going to the same place Buffy was going.

Wherever that was.

When they got there, Suz was going to do the thing

she'd wanted to do ever since she'd let Willow, Oz, and Xander take her home.

She was going to take matters into her own hands. Make up for what had happened at the Bronze.

Buffy turned the corner and Suz eased from her hiding place, then sprinted across the street, determined not to lose sight of her quarry for long.

She'd screwed things up once. She wasn't about to do it again. The pain, the humiliation of the events of earlier that evening still lodged in her chest, solid as a fist. Burning like a fireball.

Spilling her guts to Buffy had been one thing, maybe bad enough. But agreeing to let Buffy's geek friends drive her home like she was some six-year-old in need of a baby-sitter was something else entirely. Something that couldn't be taken lying down. Couldn't be left alone. She had a reputation to maintain, after all, not to mention two friends to avenge. A thing she should have already handled on her own.

But she could hardly do either once word got out she'd let Willow Rosenberg drive her home. The fact that it had actually been Oz behind the wheel wouldn't make any difference. Everyone would know that Suz Tompkins was slipping. Had slipped. She couldn't afford to let that happen.

Not at all.

She rounded a corner, then ducked down as Buffy turned her head.

Where on earth was Buffy going?

Not that it made all that much difference. Wherever Buffy went, Suz was going to follow.

The way she had it figured, it was a meeting with

whomever was really responsible for what had happened to Leila and Heidi. Because, in spite of the strange reaction of Buffy and her friends, Suz had a hard time believing her own friends had been taken out by the twin guys she'd seen earlier that night at the Bronze. They looked too young, for one thing. For another—

What had that incredibly annoying insect Xander Harris called them?

The Pillsbury Doughboys.

Errand boys, more likely, she thought. Could they have been less threatening? Suz didn't think so.

And I let them get to me, she thought.

She'd let them sneak around after her for days, giving her the wiggins so bad she'd broken one of the first rules she and her friends had ever made. She'd taken her troubles to someone who wasn't one of them: an outsider. Then she'd agreed to let Buffy handle things while she'd practically been sent home to bed.

If I'd asked Willow to come in, would she have read me a bedtime story? she wondered. While Oz and Xander prowled around in her mother's always spotless kitchen on a late-night raid for cookies. Got milk?

Could she have been more of a wimp? Not likely.

But things weren't going to end this way. Not if she had anything to say about it.

Buffy was pretty sure she was being followed.

She'd felt it as soon as she'd left the house. The sense that there were eyes upon her. That prickle right between her shoulder blades, the one that almost always meant there was someone, or something, back there. Watching. Waiting. Following.

Ordinarily, she'd have taken the time to find out who or what it was, remove the possibility of any threat. It wasn't smart to leave your back exposed. Any Slayer, and a whole lot of non-slaying people, knew that.

But that would take time, and time was a luxury. One she didn't have. For all Buffy knew, she was being followed by something deliberately sent to distract her. It was the sort of thing Giles had warned her might happen.

Do I get points off if I'm late to the trial? she wondered. Could she default, and if she could, what would happen? Would Nemesis turn Joyce over to Mrs. Walker, the vampire mother?

Buffy picked up her pace, Giles's assessment of her situation ringing in her head.

The trial wasn't likely to be fair, and it was likely to be very nasty. Or words to that effect.

Great, she thought. *Just what I need. A trial that sounds like a dentist appointment.*

She caught a glimpse of movement out of the corner of her eye and turned her head. Nothing. Either her Slayer senses were playing tricks on her, or something else was.

Don't waste time thinking about it, she told herself as she broke into a light jog. *Just keep going.*

Get to the trial. Get Mom. Get out.

Don't look back.

"I still don't like it," Willow said.

She'd taken over Buffy's job of pacing around the library. Though the Slayer had departed several minutes ago, her group of friends were still together. They were all being careful not to look toward the clock, but each knew the others were all waiting for the same thing.

For the hands to point straight up to midnight. The hour Buffy's trial was set to begin.

"You're not supposed to like it," Xander commented as Willow marched by him. He had permission to talk again, now that the actual research part of the evening was over. "It's part of the whole Powers of Darkness thing."

"I mean, we won't even know what's going on," Willow said.

Xander glanced around the library, as if seeking support. "Everybody else here with me on the Powers of *Darkness* concept?"

"I'm there," Oz said.

"Exactly!" Willow exclaimed, whirling back to him. "That's just what I'm getting at. We can't be there. We've been left behind, in the dark. In the absence of light. In the blackness that is Stygian."

"I hate that kind," Xander put in so quickly they knew he didn't know what she meant. "That kind's the absolute worst."

"And meanwhile, Buffy needs our help." Willow collapsed into the chair Buffy had used earlier, her fingers closing around the Slayer's abandoned scrunchie. "I don't like being Inactivity Girl," she said. "It's frustrating."

"Rather like being a Watcher, in fact," Giles spoke up suddenly. "Though, I do agree with you, Willow," he went on. "About the frustration, that is. Unfortunately, I'm not sure I see any way around it, given the present circumstances."

"That's just the problem. We can't see anything!" Willow wailed.

"It's midnight," Oz said.

"Well," the Slayer murmured. She stared down at the white calling card in her hand, then back up at the house. "I guess this is it."

Two thousand Elysian Fields Lane.

She should have known it would turn out to be one of those houses that always made her want to grind her teeth. A Southern California mixed message monstrosity. Before coming to Sunnydale, Buffy had never given much thought to the fact that architecture could actively inspire fear. But then those had been the old, innocent days of life in the City of Angels.

Set on one of the low hills overlooking Sunnydale, the stone walls of the vampire mother's house gleamed white, even in the middle-of-the-night darkness. Huge white columns supported a wraparound front porch, making the house look like a cross between Tara in *Gone With the Wind*, a Greek temple on industrial strength drugs, and a grinning skull.

Appropriate, Buffy thought.

Sucking in a deep breath to steady her nerves, she proceeded up the front walk, listening to the way the soles of her boots smacked against the stone. The sense that she was being followed, watched, was still with her, but she'd successfully pushed it to the back of her mind.

It was what was in front of her that was important. Even if she wasn't going to like it very much.

She reached the front porch, climbed the short flight

of steps that led onto it. As she did, the porch light winked on. Buffy threw up an arm against the sudden glare. She could feel her muscles tensing, getting ready to fight. Before her, the front door swung silently open.

Step into my parlor, said the spider to the fly.

Spiders. Yuck.

Buffy squared her shoulders, lifted her chin, and stepped across the threshold.

"Wally. Beaver, I'm home," she called out.

Nothing.

Behind her, the door slammed closed.

CHAPTER 9

In the mansion that was his refuge, the vampire named Angel stared into the fire. But he didn't see the flames, the wood being slowly devoured. What he saw was in his mind's eye: the hands of a clock, sweeping inexorably straight up toward midnight.

I had to let her go without me.

There were lots of things Angel had resigned himself to, battles he'd learned not to fight because he knew he'd never win. Being what he was—a demon with a soul—was one of them. But, no matter how many times it happened, he'd never learned to do one thing.

He'd never learned to like the fact that there were times he had to step back and watch the woman he loved walk straight into danger. Without him.

He smacked his fist against the mantel, not feeling the hard impact of the stone, just as he didn't feel the warmth of the flames in front of him. It always intrigued him that, when troubled, building a fire was one of his first impulses. An instinct for light and warmth that had never left him, even after all these years and all the things that he'd become.

Perhaps it was genetic. Some part of him so hardwired it would always remain the same. It was that basic. That primal.

It certainly didn't seem to matter that he only got half the benefit of what the fire had to offer. All of the light. None of the warmth. He was dead, had been dead for more than 200 years. There was no fire on earth that could ever warm him.

Tell me, what is it like to be what you are and have a soul?

Against his will, his felt his lips curve upward in a bitter smile. He had to give Nemesis this much. She did know how to ask a question.

Try hell, he thought. The only thing that stopped it from being a living hell was the fact that he wasn't.

Without warning, his head swiveled, turning from the fire seconds before he heard the first of the frantic pounding on his massive front door. He crossed the room with quick, long strides, jerked the door open.

Willow was standing in the darkness of the front walkway.

Oz was beside her. Xander and Giles just behind. He could see both Oz's van and Giles's battered Citroën parked beside the curb.

Hail, hail, the gang's all here, Angel thought. The only question was, why had they come?

"What is it?" he asked, his voice sharp. "What's gone wrong?"

"Nothing," Willow answered. In her hands, she held a large copper bowl.

"Well, you didn't come all the way over here just to fix me a midnight snack, did you?"

Oz lifted an object in his right hand: a jug of spring water.

"Scrying spell," he said shortly.

Angel's eyebrows rose. He never underestimated the strength of the feelings Buffy's friends had for her, but that wasn't the same as saying they couldn't still surprise him.

"Scrying spell," he echoed. "Interesting idea." He looked back at Willow. "Yours?"

The redhead nodded, her arms tightening around the bowl. "I thought if we couldn't go with Buffy, at least we could see what was going on. That way, we could—you know—if something goes wrong."

"Make like the cavalry," Angel suggested.

Once more, Willow nodded. "Something like that," she acknowledged.

"I have explained the risks," Giles put in, his voice slightly wooden. "But it appears I'm to be overruled, as always."

And not just about casting the spell itself, Angel thought. Giles could hardly be thrilled about the location Willow had chosen. *But he'd come, for the same reason I'll let him in.*

Because the Slayer came first. Always.

Angel stepped back, gesturing for Buffy's friends to enter.

"Come in," he said. And tried not to care about the fact that Giles was the last to cross the threshold.

* * *

"Mom?"

Buffy stood just inside the door of the vampire's house, making a quick assessment of her surroundings. She was in a marble entryway, with halls moving off it in either direction, like outstretched arms. In front of her was a wall covered in wallpaper decorated with enormous cabbage roses.

It seemed the vampire mother's attachment to flowers wasn't limited to her clothing.

And if that wasn't enough to make a girl worry about what was coming next, Buffy didn't know what was.

She pulled in a breath, held it for a moment, then expelled it. The air of the house was stale and cold.

It's been a long time since anything alive has come here, Buffy thought.

And anything that had hadn't lived very long.

Just thinking about that kicked her pulse up a full notch.

Where's my mom?

Deciding that picking a direction, any direction, was better than standing still, the Slayer chose the hallway to her right. She began to ease herself along it, keeping her back to the wall.

"Oh, good," a voice to her left said. "You're on time." Shifting instantly into a battle crouch, Buffy whirled back toward the entry hall. Nemesis was standing in the middle of it. All three faces Buffy could see were smiling.

"That's good," the Balancer said, her heads nodding to show her approval. "I like promptness in a participant. It bodes well for the trial."

Buffy felt her hold on her temper start to slip away from her. She was here to save her mother's life, and this four-faced walking testament to the benefits of going in for a regular facial was making it sound as if Buffy was a contestant on some lame game show.

"Where's my mom?"

Nemesis's ugly smile got a little wider. "Temper, temper," she said. "Patience is a virtue, Slayer. Just ask your Watcher."

Buffy bit down hard on the tip of her tongue. She should know better than to let this agent of the Powers of Darkness taunt her. It was a potential distraction, just as Giles had warned her. She had to keep her wits about her. Focus on what was most important.

Get the details of the trial. Get Mom. Get out.

"Where's the vampire mother, Mrs. Walker?"

"So you discovered who she is," Nemesis commented. "I wondered if you'd bother. That was fast work. Good for you."

"Where is she?" Buffy asked again.

"Nowhere that need concern you," answered the Balancer. "She has no part in what is about to befall you. Once she agreed to the terms of the trial, her role was complete. Now all she can do is wait for the outcome."

"She's going to be real disappointed."

"We shall see, won't we?" asked the Balancer. "Now, if you'll just walk this way—"

"After you," Buffy said.

Nemesis smiled again, then turned to move off down the left-hand corridor. Buffy followed slowly, her eyes constantly darting from left to right to take in as much information as she could about her surroundings.

With every step she took, Buffy grew more and more aware of how still and silent the house was. No sounds from outside penetrated its thick walls. No sounds carried from elsewhere inside. The only sounds Buffy heard were her own breathing. Her own footsteps. The steady, heavy beating of her own heart.

For the first time, Buffy realized that, when she wasn't speaking, Nemesis made no sound at all.

The wall with the cabbage rose wallpaper ended in an entrance to a sunken living room. The wallpaper there was covered with giant purple irises.

"This trial wouldn't have anything to do with my ability to redecorate, would it?" she inquired.

All four of Nemesis's faces gave a short bark of laughter. The red eyes glowed.

The furniture in the living room looked old-fashioned, like maybe the vampire mother, Mrs. Walker, was still hauling around her furnishings from the Civil War. Straight-backed sofas. Spindle-legged tables and chairs. All of it looked uncomfortable. Except for the lamps, there were no modern appliances anywhere that Buffy could see. No stereo. No TV, or VCR.

No wonder Webster and Percy turned out to be such losers, Buffy thought. Not much to do for entertainment around this place but bite people. And then you didn't even get to put your feet up on the furniture when you were done.

"The main part of the house is quite spacious, as you can see," Nemesis said as she led Buffy diagonally across the living room to a doorway on the far side.

"You know," Buffy commented, as she followed Nemesis across a carpet just a few shades lighter than the purple flowers on the walls, "if this Powers of Darkness thing ever stops being fun, I'll bet you could have a bright new future in real estate."

And could we please just get on with the trial?

"I am hardly your concern," Nemesis pronounced as Buffy trailed her into a spacious kitchen whose wallpaper was decorated with what Willow had once pointed out was a poisonous flower. Foxglove.

Nemesis crossed to the far side of the room, making for one of two doors which stood side by side.

Now we get to it, Buffy thought. *The lady, or the tiger?*

"What concerns you," Nemesis said, "is right in *here*."

She whipped one of the doors open. Buffy tensed, then did a double take.

"I'm supposed to look for my mother in a broom closet?"

Nemesis slammed the door with a force that had the botanical dinner plates mounted on the wall rattling in their flowered holders.

"I hate it when that happens," she said. She took two steps to the left. "What *really* concerns you is down here."

Triumphantly, she opened the second door. Buffy could see a set of shadowy stairs, leading downward into darkness.

Another basement. Figures, Buffy thought. How come she never got to fight something that liked to hang out aboveground? Like, say, for instance, in the park. In the daytime. With the birdies tweeting in the background.

Buffy moved to the top of the steps and peered down. The rest of the vampire mother's house was spotless, not a speck of dust anywhere. But the stairs leading down to the basement were thick with it, the rafters above them festooned with cobwebs.

"Once you set foot on those stairs," Nemesis said, "you have entered the world of the trial and left the world you know behind."

Great, Buffy thought. If that wasn't anything more than a fancy way of saying "all bets are off," she didn't know what was.

"So what's down there?" she inquired. "Monsters?"

Nemesis nodded. "Got it in one. Though the kind depends entirely on you."

Buffy rolled her eyes. She should have known better than to ask a straight question. These days, a girl just never got a straight answer from anything over 300 years old.

"Listen carefully and hear the terms of your trial," the Balancer intoned. "Your adversary has called upon the Powers of Darkness to avenge the deaths of her—"

"I know that. I was there for that part," Buffy interrupted.

"Silence!" Nemesis roared.

"Sorry," Buffy mumbled.

"Your adversary has shown remarkable familial devotion," Nemesis continued. Buffy tried not to notice how much she sounded like Giles. "Particularly for a vampire. Rather than abandon her sons, or kill them outright, she changed them herself and has kept them with her all these years. In her own way, she loves them.

"Your trial will determine whose love is stronger, the vampire mother's for her sons, or yours for your mother."

Well that should be a no-brainer, Buffy thought. She could feel herself begin to relax for the first time since entering the vampire mother's house.

If determining whose love was stronger, Buffy's or Vamp Mama's, then Buffy figured she ought to win this trial, hands down.

She was human. Mrs. Walker was not. She was a vampire, a thing without a soul. Surely what she felt for her sons couldn't begin to compare or compete with the way Buffy felt about Joyce. Mrs. Walker had lost her capacity for real love long ago.

"If your love is the stronger," Nemesis went on, "then it, and you, will triumph. Mrs. Walker's call for vengeance will be denied. You will find your mother, free her, and return to the upper world, the world you know. The two of you will then leave this place unharmed."

"Seems like an awful lot of trouble for a predictable outcome," Buffy remarked. "I'm human; she's not. End of story. Simple plot."

Nemesis's smile was predatory. "You think so?" she inquired. "I would have thought that you of all people would have realized by now that nothing is simple when it comes to love."

Without warning, the Slayer felt a chill pass over her. *It's true,* she thought. Images of the people she loved, who'd claimed to love her, danced across her mind.

Her friends, who were always there for her. Her father, who had been once. Her mother. Giles. And finally Angel, least simple of all. Even when he'd lost his soul and gone back to being Angelus, she and Angel had still been bound together. He'd proved it himself. She'd been the one he'd wanted to hurt the most.

"What happens if I fail?" she inquired.

Nemesis's red eyes regarded her steadily. "I don't really have to answer that question, do I?"

"I guess not."

"In that case, this phase of the proceedings is officially over. You are cleared to proceed to the trial. Get ready."

"Wait a minute!" Buffy protested.

"Get set."

"But what about—"

Nemesis reached out with one enormous hand and gave the Slayer a shove. Buffy stumbled down the stairs, her fingers desperately seeking for purchase on the handrail, her feet raising clouds of dust.

"Go!" the Balancer shouted.

Then she slammed the door, plunging Buffy into complete and utter darkness.

CHAPTER 10

It had taken Suz two complete circuits of the house to find out everything she wanted to know.

First on the list had been the fact that, in spite of its up-scale location, the house Buffy had entered didn't seem to have an alarm system. Second was the fact that a series of windows at the back of the house seemed to lead to one big room spanning the length of the main floor.

The room beyond the windows seemed to glow softly, illuminated by something Suz hadn't quite been able to identify. She'd thought it was candles at first, momentarily wondering if she'd misjudged the reason Buffy had left her own house in the middle of the night. Maybe the spirits she intended to raise were the romantic kind.

Then Suz had realized the light was too even to be candlelight. It didn't waver or flicker. It burned steady and low. It was just one more mystery in a night full of them. From her hiding place, the shadow of a big tree in the backyard, Suz felt her determination grow.

She didn't like mysteries. She liked things up front, spelled out, in the open, where you could look them in the eye as you took them down. It was the things you couldn't see, the things you didn't know about, that could hurt you.

I'm not leaving till I find out what's going on.

Suz shifted position, eyes glued to the house. Any minute now. She'd been watching for about fifteen minutes after Buffy'd gone in. In that time, Suz had seen no movement at all. Nobody going in. Nobody coming out. No one even moving around, as far as she could tell. If she hadn't seen the door swing open and Buffy go in herself, Suz would have figured there was nobody home.

Fine. The fewer people there were inside, the fewer she'd have to beat the snot out of to get the answers that she wanted.

Okay, enough waiting. Now it's show time.

Satisfied that the room she'd targeted was empty, Suz began to move forward, keeping her body low. She stayed in the reaching shadow of the tree for as long as she could. When it ended, she sprinted for the back of the house. Plastering her back against it beside two of the windows, she waited for her pulse to slow.

She hadn't come this far to give herself away by being a mouth-breather now.

Just call me Suz Tompkins, Commando.

When her breath was quiet and even again, Suz crouched down beside the window she'd chosen, considering her options. *I might as well try the simplest approach first.* One of the few classes she'd actually liked had been sophomore geometry. The shortest distance between two points is a straight line.

Angling her head away from the window, she reached out with one arm and gave the window a quick shove upward, then whipped her arm back.

The window slid open, silently.

Suz felt her heart give a leap of triumph even as she held her body motionless. That had been awfully easy. Maybe too. In Suz's experience, things that looked too good to be true usually were.

She waited. Nothing happened. Finally, she decided she'd waited long enough. With a quick surge of movement, she thrust one leg over the window sill, ducked her head in, then pivoted and brought the other leg inside. She stood up and turned to face the window once more.

Swiftly Suz lowered it back into position, leaving a gap just wide enough for her to get her fingers through at the bottom. She didn't want to take time to discover if all the windows were unlocked as well, and this was as good a way as any to identify the one she'd come through.

She turned around, adrenaline coursing through her.

I've done it. I'm in.

"You're absolutely certain you want to do this," Giles said, his tone hovering between a statement and a question.

On the opposite side of the fireplace, Willow nodded vigorously, her red hair swinging. "Absolutely. Positive."

The group was standing in what Giles supposed he should consider Angel's living room. *Can one have a living room if one is dead?*

A useless exercise to ponder such a question, of course, but still, it served to keep his mind off one thing.

I'd rather be anywhere than here. Within reason, of course.

Still, Giles's sense of fairness forced him to admit, if only to himself, that Angel had already been helpful. He'd stoked the fire, making it burn clear and hot, just the way it ought to for the first phase of the spell. *I suppose I ought to feel grateful for Angel's assistance.*

Not very likely, all in all.

Standing with Xander on one side of the fireplace, Giles studied Willow, as she stood just opposite. She looked nervous, but determined. Silent as usual, Oz stood beside her. Angel stood alone, back from the fire between the two groups. The point of the triangle. The fulcrum.

Those of us who willingly seek the vampire's help on one side, and those who don't on the other, thought Giles.

Though he'd done his best to come up with an alternative, Giles had to admit that Willow's plan to cast a scrying spell was a sound, though dangerous, one. He'd even go so far as to admit perhaps he should have thought of it himself. He just wished Willow hadn't insisted the spell be cast at Angel's mansion. Giles didn't like asking Angel for help. It went against every instinct he had, every rule he'd ever learned.

The fact that he was the Watcher to a Slayer who'd pretty much broken every rule in the book wasn't helping any, but then it seldom did. Particularly when one of the biggest rules she broke on a regular basis was a pretty basic one: never trust a vampire. Let alone love one.

Vampires were the enemy. Good only for one thing:

staking. Though even Giles had to admit Angel was hardly ordinary, as vampires went.

Still, he'd had a difficult enough time trusting Angel before his unfortunate return engagement as Angelus. It was almost impossible to trust him now, after what he'd done to Jenny Calendar.

And thinking that way puts your needs first, Rupert, he reminded himself. Which meant he was breaking a rule of his own.

The needs of the Slayer came first. Always.

"All right, then," he said, looking again toward Willow. "Since you're so determined, we might as well get on with this, I suppose. You have the herbs to purify the room?"

Willow nodded once more and moved to a low table Angel had placed in front of the fire. On it was the collection of items needed to cast the scrying spell.

A bundle of sage. A clear quartz crystal as long and thick as Giles's forefinger. The jug of spring water and the copper bowl. The book that contained the scrying spell. Angel had also supplied a cushion for Willow to sit on. In order for the spell to work, she had to hold the bowl.

"I've said this before, but I think it bears repeating," Giles said as Willow picked up the bundle of sage and moved toward the fire. "Scrying spells are very powerful things, definitely not to be undertaken lightly. Casting a spell of this nature takes absolute concentration at all times. One slip—"

"And we'll be no worse off than we are right now," Angel broke in, breaking his long silence. "The spell can't change what's happening to Buffy, Giles; it can only show us what it is."

"I don't need you to—" Giles came back hotly. He broke off, inhaled a slow, deep breath.

Arguing with Angel was hardly useful. Particularly when he was right. So far.

"I am aware that the spell won't impact Buffy," he said. "It's the impact on Willow I'm worried about. Scrying isn't like other spells. The person casting the spell, the scryer, for lack of a better term, doesn't just summon energy, bring it into being. She literally becomes the conduit for the energy itself. There are historical accounts of scryers being driven mad by the power of what they summoned."

Giles took his glasses off, wiped the lenses, then settled them back onto his face again.

"Are we all clear on my concerns now?"

"Giles, I have to do this," Willow said after a moment. "It's . . . a . . ." her forehead wrinkled, as if she were searching for the right words to convince him. "Thing I have to do. For Buffy."

"That clears that up," Xander muttered, putting in his two cents for the first time since he'd arrived.

Giles sighed. *Well, I tried.* And now he would do his best. As always.

"You have some personal item of Buffy's? You'll need that to focus the images you summon."

The redhead dug into her jacket pocket and produced the scrunchie Buffy had pulled from her hair during their research session in the library earlier that night.

"Okay, so it's not a personality-filled personal item," she acknowledged. "But it'll work. I know it will."

"If you say so." He moved the table and picked up the book that contained the scrying spell.

"Everybody ready? Right. Let's begin with purifying the room."

Willow cast the bundle of sage into the flames.

"Whoa," Xander said. "Nobody told me it would smell like spaghetti."

I can do this.

In front of Angel's fire, Willow sat cross-legged on the cushion he'd provided, holding the copper bowl between her knees. To one side of her, Oz stood ready with the jug of spring water. One in each hand, Willow held the quartz crystal and Buffy's hair tie. Giles stood behind her, ready to prompt her with the words of the spell, if she should need it.

Hardly.

She was about to call upon Isis, an ancient deity so powerful she'd brought her murdered husband, Osiris, back to life.

One doesn't forget to ask a girl like that nicely.

"Okay," Willow said. "I'm ready."

She cupped the quartz in her hands, breathed on it, then placed it in the bottom of the bowl. At her nod, Oz poured in the spring water. Willow waited until the water in the bowl was still enough so that she could see the crystal in the bottom clearly. Then she cast the scrunchie on top of the water, trying not to notice the way it floated like a tiny fabric doughnut.

"Mighty Isis, Giver of Life. Hear my plea."

Willow bent and blew upon the surface of the water, making it ripple. Slowly, the scrunchie sank to the bottom. Once more, she waited until the surface of the water was still.

"Breathe life into the image of the one I call."

A shower of sparks shot from the fireplace as a gust of wind roared down the chimney, then flowed over Willow. The surface of the water roiled.

"Hear now the name I give," Willow called out.

The room became completely still. The surface of the water, smooth as glass. The air above it began to shimmer, ever so slightly. As if just waiting for Willow to say the words that would make it coalesce, give it a true form and substance.

"Buffy Summers."

Buffy stood at the top of the basement stairs, coughing to clear the dust from her lungs, waiting for her eyes to adjust to the darkness.

Talk about a lost cause.

The darkness was total. Absolute.

Why didn't I bring a flashlight? the Slayer wondered. *Well, gee, if I'd known the trial was going to consist of being shut up in a pitch dark otherworldly-type basement, I probably would have,* she thought.

But she hadn't known. And she'd wanted to leave her hands free for whatever came at her. Though, at the moment, the thing that looked most likely was giant dust bunnies.

Gripping the handrail tightly with her right hand, her left hand extended out in front of her, Buffy started down. Every sense she had screamed at her to hurry, but she forced herself to go slowly, testing each step in front of her with her foot before she put her weight on it.

If ever she was going to make Giles proud of her by using the power of her Slayer's brain as well as the strength of her fists, Buffy figured now would be the time.

The stairs had looked solid, as far as Buffy'd been able to see them. Which hadn't actually been that far. She could hardly save her mother if she injured herself by losing her footing and tumbling to the bottom.

Always assuming that there is one. This wasn't a normal basement, after all.

Buffy took another step down. Light as gossamer, sticky as flypaper, something brushed against her outstretched left hand. She jerked it back before she could help herself. The thing that had brushed against it came too, settling in a great clinging cloud over Buffy's head, sticking to her hair and eyelashes.

Cobwebs. Gross.

Quickly, Buffy brushed them away, wishing once more that she had a source of light. It was going to be a pretty tedious trip if she had to feel her way through the basement with her hands in front of her the whole time.

"You idiot," she said suddenly.

She had a source of light, in her own jacket pocket. The one thing she'd brought along. It might not be all that powerful, but it was a whole lot better than the nothing she had going for her right now.

Quickly, Buffy dug out the book of matches she'd taken from the living room mantel. She eased the matchbox open, careful to keep it cupped in one palm. It was so dark, she couldn't even see the box, couldn't tell which side was up. The last thing she needed was to spill her matches down the stairs before she'd even managed to light one.

Her fingers found a match. Got it out. She slid the box lid closed, located the match tip by feel, then ran the fat knob down the rough side of the box. The match caught the very first time. Buffy breathed a sigh of relief. It wasn't a lot of light, but it was enough.

She slipped the box of matches back into her pocket and lifted the lit match, high.

Above the feeble golden glow of the match, a pair of eyes the color of split pea soup was staring down.

"Buffy!" Willow cried. "Look out!"

She could feel the energy of the scrying spell pouring through her. A headache pounded, right behind her eyes. But she knew she couldn't look away from the image she'd helped conjure. If she did, she could break the spell.

"What is that thing in there with her?" she heard Xander mutter. "The Jolly Green Giant? A guy like that should be on our side, shouldn't he?"

"It's big," Oz agreed.

There's nothing I can do! Willow thought. She couldn't help her friend. She could only watch.

The image moved slowly, at times making Buffy appear frozen.

Am I doing that? Can I make it go faster?

"Is this the part where I get why those historical guys went crazy?" she asked aloud.

She felt Oz's hands descend upon her shoulders.

"Steady," he said quietly.

"You don't have to continue, you know, Willow," Giles answered from his place beside her. "We can end this at any time. Buffy wouldn't want you to risk yourself unnecessarily."

But this is necessary, Willow thought. Buffy's friends, her support team, needed to know what was happening to her. *And I'm the one who can show them.*

"It's all right," she said. "I can keep going."

"Buffy's a fighter," Angel said. "She'll think of something."

She knew that.

"I know that."

Come on, Buffy. Think of something.

She did the first thing she could think of.

Her Slayer's instincts sizzling through her like a thousand volts of electricity, Buffy bent her knees and jumped. A split second before it burned out, she buried the flaming tip of the match in one of the bright green eyes above her.

An agonized howl split the air of the basement. Instantly, the eye winked out. Buffy landed hard, felt the step begin to give way beneath her. She stumbled several steps forward, her hands clutching for purchase on the handrail.

She felt herself slam into something thick and fuzzy. It howled again. Buffy felt long claws scrabble against her shoulder. She jerked back, turned her body sideways, put both hands on the rail, then leaped up, kicking out with both feet. She felt her heavy boots connect. With another howl, the thing fell backward down the stairs. Buffy heard a bone-breaking crunch as the whatever-it-was hit bottom.

That's one question solved, at least. Now I know there is a bottom.

Then, to her astonishment, the thing burst into flames. The acrid smell of burning dust filled the Slayer's nostrils. It smelled exactly the way the heater did when her mom turned it on for the first time every winter.

Maybe she hadn't been so wrong about those giant dust bunnies.

Buffy held her position on the staircase, one hand raised to shield her face from the flames, as the thing at the bottom of the stairs blazed like a bonfire.

Flame retardant not, she thought.

It had stopped howling by now, so she was pretty certain that it was dead. Buffy hadn't worn her watch, but she figured she'd taken care of whatever this was in under a minute. If this was as good as Nemesis could dish out, the trial would be over in next to no time.

And wouldn't that be just dandy?

Not only that, the thing she'd killed was actually going to help her in her quest to find her mother.

The blazing pile at the bottom of the stairs was a little smaller now. The thing's death-throes thrashings had caused it to roll to one side. Now Buffy could get to the bottom of the stairs, and beyond, without actually having to walk across hot coals. She appreciated that. The boots were pretty new. Not only that, she really liked them. She'd just as soon not do anything that would cause the soles to do a tuna melt if she could help it.

Buffy sprinted down the staircase. At the bottom of the stairs, she paused. She turned back, raised one foot, and brought it down on the bottom stair. Hard.

Again, again the Slayer slammed her foot against the stair tread. On the third try, the wood of the stair cracked, then splintered, then broke apart. Buffy stomped once more, just for good measure, then knelt and selected a couple of likely stakes from the pile. She thrust them into her empty jacket pocket.

Hey. Why not?

The rules of the trial had said she couldn't *bring* any weapons, but they hadn't set any restrictions on picking up or even creating weapons as she went along.

Xander had made her watch enough "Star Trek" that she'd seen the episode where Captain Kirk battled a reptile captain on an alien desert planet. He'd made gunpowder and a hand-held cannon, for crying out loud.

Buffy bent once more, retrieved the largest of the pieces of wood, then straightened and turned around. The flames of the monster dust bunny had settled down to a cheerful campfire sort of glow.

And here I am, without the makings for s'mores.

Feeling confident now, Buffy strode forward and thrust the end of her board into the fire, holding it there until it caught. She knew her improvised torch wouldn't last long, but it was a whole lot better than carrying a match around. At least now she could see a little more of where she was going.

"Thanks for the light."

Then, holding her torch up like she was doing her best imitation of the Statue of Liberty, the Slayer moved forward into the darkness of the basement.

Hold on. I'm coming, Mom.

CHAPTER 11

Suz was in a portrait gallery. It made no sense at all. Portrait galleries were for museums, not people's houses. Unless maybe you were royalty or something.

Is there royalty in Sunnydale?

She didn't think so.

But at least now she understood where the strange light she'd noticed from outside had come from.

Each portrait was illuminated by a long cylindrical brass light. One on the top. One on the bottom. They cast arcs of light up or down onto the canvases, highlighting a face, a hand. Leaving the rest in shadow.

What is with this place? she wondered.

In spite of her desire to get other kinds of answers, she moved closer. This was her greatest asset, her biggest drawback. The thing that nobody had ever really understood about her.

Her curiosity.

And it almost always got her into trouble.

It wasn't so much a desire to rebel that made Suz Tompkins incapable of coloring inside the lines, but a desire to know more about the nature of boundaries. How far could something, someone, be made to bend?

There was really only one way to find out.

You had to push until either the thing you leaned against gave way. Or you did.

Drawn to what she saw on the walls, Suz moved to stand in front of the largest of the paintings. It was the portrait of a soldier.

Confederate, she thought. The artist had even painted the rebel's red flag streaming out against a blue sky in the background.

"Handsome, isn't he?" a voice said. Suz started. She whirled around, instantly assuming a battle crouch.

Is there a limit to my stupidity? she wondered.

She'd trailed Buffy for blocks, successfully broken into the house after her, then left her back exposed. So much for curiosity. It had killed the cat.

It can just as easily kill you, you know.

Not that she'd go without a fight, of course.

The question was, would she have to? Suz studied the woman in front of her through narrowed eyes.

She was big, that much was for sure. But she looked big and soft. She was dressed up, like she'd just come from a funeral parlor, or the opera. Basic black and pearls. Suz already knew that she was quiet. So quiet she hadn't even heard her come into the room.

When was the last time somebody'd managed to

sneak up on her? Suz couldn't remember. But it had to be years now.

The woman didn't look like she was about to attack. She just stood there. *She's not so tough,* Suz thought. Even though there was a lot of her. *If I have to, I can take her down.*

She allowed herself to relax, just a little. *Keep her talking. Find out what makes her tick,* she thought. She'd talked herself out of plenty of tough spots. There was no reason to think she couldn't do the same with this one. Besides, she had to figure the woman wanted something from her, or she'd have raised the alarm by now.

Suz turned back to the portrait, keeping her body loose, weight poised over the balls of her feet just in case she had to run. She kept her voice easy as she answered.

"I always like a man in uniform. Who was he?"

The woman stepped up beside her. Suz shifted one gliding step away, but the woman in black made no attempt to follow. Instead, she stood still, gazing at the portrait.

"My husband. But I'm forgetting my manners," she went on, before Suz could even think of a comment. "Allow me to introduce myself. I'm Zahalia Walker."

She extended one hand.

"Suz Tompkins," Suz mumbled. *What have I gotten myself into?* she wondered. And how soon could she get back out?

She shook the hand the older woman offered. The fingers were soft and limp, like clutching a handful of cold spaghetti.

"So," Suz said. "Was that your husband's Halloween costume or something?"

"Don't be ridiculous," Zahalia Walker snapped. Her accent might be as Southern as it could get, but the tone sounded exactly like Suz's own mother when she was pissed about something. Which was pretty much all the time.

Just what I need. A scolding from Miz Scarlett.

"We had that portrait commissioned as soon as he enlisted. It was finished the day before he left home."

"And that would have been in—"

"Eighteen sixty-one."

I had to ask, didn't I?

She was doing it again. Asking one more question. Why couldn't she just leave well enough alone?

Either this woman was totally insane, or she was a first-rate con artist playing some weird game that was all her own. As far as Suz could tell, she was absolutely serious. The expression on her face hadn't changed at all.

Remind me never to ask you to play a game of poker, Suz thought. Not that she and this woman were likely to be doing much socializing.

"Being made an officer was his proudest moment," Mrs. Walker went on. She shifted her gaze from the portrait to Suz, her eyes suddenly sharp. "After the birth of our sons, of course."

Suz felt a strange prickling sensation travel across the surface of her skin.

Sons.

Don't do it, she told herself. *Don't ask. You don't really want to know.*

Oh, but she did, she thought. Wasn't this the reason she'd followed Buffy in the first place?

"Twins?" she heard herself say aloud.

"Why, yes," Zahalia Walker answered, her Southern accent becoming even more pronounced. She smiled, displaying a mouthful of gleaming white teeth. "Did you know my boys?"

Did, Suz thought. Past tense. What on earth had Buffy done?

"I don't think so."

"Oh, but I think you did," Zahalia Walker countered. She took a step closer. Suz shifted back. "I think that's why you're here tonight. You've come to cheer the Slayer on. I won't ask how you got in. It really doesn't matter. The fact that you're here at all could be considered a violation of the terms of the trial. In which case, I've already won."

Trial? Abruptly, the prickle on Suz's skin turned into a thing that crawled. This woman *was* insane.

"I don't know what you're talking about."

"Don't you?"

Once more, Zahalia Walker smiled. Then, before Suz had time to blink, one hand shot out to grip her elbow. Hard. She discovered that the fleshy, white fingers that had felt so useless just a moment before had the strength to press skin down to the bone.

Suz lashed out with her free arm, only to have it gripped and held as tightly as the other one was.

"In that case, there are all sorts of things that you don't know about, sugar," said Zahalia Walker.

Before Suz's horrified eyes, the woman's forehead folded, and her eyes turned yellow. Her teeth became . . . something Suz didn't really want to explore.

Things like this aren't supposed to exist. They can't exist!

"But you will," Zahalia Walker whispered through her long, sharp teeth. "I promise."

All right. What now?

The basement echoed with the *clomp* of Buffy's boots as she explored. She was moving along the basement's perimeter. Her left hand holding the torch, her right brushing against the wall. She'd decided to be organized.

It was a little like taking one of the aptitude tests she dimly recalled from grade school. In a total-body-experience kind of way.

"If you wanted to determine what was inside this shape, how would you do it?" she could still remember the guidance counselor asking. She could also remember taking the yellow number-two pencil in her hand, tracing the shape of the triangle over and over. Start at the outside edge. Work your way in.

Miss nothing. Find my mom.

Unfortunately, the only things she'd found so far were more dust. And more dark.

How long have I been walking?

"Mom?" she called out. "Mom, can you hear me? Where are you?"

What if I can't find her?

Buffy began to walk faster, the fingers of her right hand scraping as she ran them against the basement wall. She held her torch a little higher, extending it out, trying to see a little farther into the darkness. Her ears strained to hear any sound. The sense of urgency grew with every step she took.

Mom! Where are you?

"Mom!" she called again. "Mom, answer me!"

No answer. Silence.

Buffy reached a corner, turned left. Began to run.

Why couldn't her mother answer? Was she injured? Dying? What if Buffy couldn't get to her in time?

If she failed. If she lost.

Stop it! she told herself fiercely. *Just stop it.*

Now was hardly the time to wallow in self-doubt. She could do that any night of the week, down at the Bronze.

Couldn't things have been easy, just this once? Why did her life always have to be so hard? A simple vamp staking. Now that was a thing she always understood, one she could really go for right about now.

Without warning, the fingers of Buffy's right hand extended into empty space as the basement opened out. Buffy pivoted swiftly, acting on pure Slayer's instinct, her right hand searching for the wall.

Before it got there, a hand snaked out of the darkness, seized her by the wrist, and dragged her forward.

"No!" Willow sobbed.

Angel took one look at the redhead's pale features and decided enough was enough. He pulled Giles aside.

Going to Giles wasn't necessarily his first choice, but if ever there was somebody who'd learned when what he wanted came first and when it didn't, Angel had to figure he was the guy.

"I don't like this," he said in a low voice. "It's not getting us anywhere. All we're doing is torturing ourselves, Willow most of all. I don't think she can take much more."

"Yes, well, for once I actually agree with you," Giles nodded. "The question is, can we get her to re-

lease the spell? I don't have to tell you how determined she can be."

No, you don't, Angel thought. Willow's tenacity in
the face of danger had impressed him more than
once.

"What about Oz?"

"Good thought—"

"All right!"

Angel and Giles both turned their attention back to
the group before the fire at the sound of Xander's en-
thusiastic voice.

"It was a vamp," he explained. "She dusted him.
That's two for our side. What are you guys doing over
there? You're missing all the best parts. There's no instant replay on this, you know."

"It's not a game," Angel said. "Not for Buffy."

"I know that," Xander came right back. "You don't
have to act like you know everything just because
you're older."

"Stop it!" Willow cried, staring into the bowl. "Don't
fight. It only makes things worse. My head . . . it hurts
so much."

"Willow," Giles said urgently. He moved to kneel beside her. "I know you want to watch out for Buffy, but
are you sure you should go on? The spell is already a
serious drain on your energy. Trying to maintain it
could . . . injure your mind."

Willow's eyes never wavered from the image of the
Slayer. "If Buffy can keep going, then so can I."

Not a fair comparison, Angel thought.

"Will," Oz said. "Buffy's the Slayer. You're you. Not
equal things. You should listen to Giles."

"Later," Willow said through gritted teeth. "Not yet. Please, Giles."

"Very well," Giles said. "But next time, I make the call."

"What's that?" Xander asked suddenly.

"It looks like—" Oz said.

"No, it can't be," Willow interrupted.

"It doesn't make any sense," Angel said.

Giles snorted. "Since when has that stopped her?"

In the air above the water, an image of Cordelia Chase was forming.

"I know what you are," Suz said. "You're a vampire."

She was trying to hang tough, but it was difficult. First she'd been dragged by her hair into the living room. Now the thing that called herself Zahalia Walker was tying her to a sofa.

"Very good," Zahalia said, as she gave the rope one last vicious tug. Suz tried to ignore the way it dug into her legs, cutting off circulation. The vampire mother grinned, exposing that truly revolting set of teeth. "Are you frightened?"

Think about it.

Suz was only human, after all. Which was more than she could say for the thing looming over her.

"Try revolted. Just like I was by your boys."

"Don't you talk about my sons that way," snarled Zahalia Walker. "They were fine boys." A look of cunning appeared in her beady yellow eyes. "They were good to me," she went on. "They always brought their food home to meet their mother. The last two looked an awful lot like you. Maybe they were friends of yours."

Suz could feel her body start to shake. Anger. Disgust. Horror. She'd been right. She'd known it. Leila and Heidi were dead. But not even in her worst nightmare would Suz ever have conjured up this end.

What did it feel like to have the blood drained out of you?

Not a great time for her curiosity to surface, she thought. Particularly since she was all too likely to find out the answer.

"I'm going to enjoy watching you die," she said. "If Buffy doesn't kill you, I will."

The vampire mother threw back her head and roared with laughter. "And how will you manage that, I wonder? No, no. Don't tell me. I just love a good surprise. That's the only reason you're still alive, honey. You're my own special little surprise package for the Slayer.

"Of course, the surprise will be that you *are* alive."

Oh, God, Suz thought. She began to writhe against the ropes that held her.

The vampire mother laughed once more. She reached for Suz's head, held it still.

"Don't worry, this won't hurt a bit," she promised.

Suz felt something sharp and hot pierce her throat.

And then the darkness swallowed her.

CHAPTER 12

"Cordy?"

Buffy stared at the figure that was slowly materializing out of nowhere before her, illuminated by the light of her fitful torch.

The torch was definitely a little worse for wear after Buffy's recent encounter with the vampire. She'd had to use the end of the torch to dust it when the vamp refused to release her other arm.

Actually, the torch wasn't the only thing a little worse for wear. Cordy had also looked better. From what Buffy could see. She was tied to a chair. Or actually, a throne. Held in place by ropes crisscrossing her chest and wrapped around her wrists. On her head rested a beauty queen crown. She was dressed like she was going to a prom.

Her head was dropped forward, her chin resting on

her chest. And staining the pale fabric of her pale formal dress was . . .

Blood.

No! That's not the way it happened! Buffy thought.

Cordelia had been tied up like this the time Marcie Ross had kidnapped her, determined to make Cordy pay for what she'd done.

Or, more specifically, what she hadn't. Which had been to notice Marcie was alive. Marcie Ross had literally turned invisible, her fellow students at Sunnydale High had ignored her for so long.

But it didn't end this way, Buffy thought. Cautiously, she moved forward. Buffy had rescued Cordelia moments before Marcie had made good on her threat to give Cordy a brand new look. Courtesy of the business end of a scalpel.

Slowly, Buffy reached out and eased Cordy's face up. Her eyes were closed, as if to deny the fact that Marcie had been more successful this time.

New eyebrows arched up into Cordy's forehead. A series of fine lines like two new sets of lower eyelashes had been etched into the hollows beneath her eyes. The corners of her mouth curved up, up, up until they met her cheekbones.

She looked like a mutilated clown.

Without warning, Cordelia's eyes flew open. Buffy jolted back a step, releasing her hold.

"Look at me," Cordelia said, her voice raspy but just as sharp as ever. "This is all your fault. You didn't stop her in time."

"But I did," Buffy protested. "I did stop her. Don't you remember?"

I didn't lose. I won.

"Then how do you explain this?" Cordelia asked.

You tell me.

"What's *that?*" Cordelia asked suddenly.

"What's what?"

"That thing behind you."

Buffy spun around. Something was rolling toward her out of the darkness of the basement.

Something of the severed head variety. It bumped against her legs and stopped, face up.

"Xander?" Buffy said.

What in the hell was going on?

She'd prevented this too, hadn't she? Xander hadn't actually become the victim of Ms. French, substitute biology teacher, a.k.a. the man-killing She-Mantis. She of the ability to literally make guys' heads spin.

Though that probably had to do with the fact that she was taking them off at the time.

But I won this fight, too, Buffy thought. *What is this? Some sort of twisted Buffy Summers, This Is Your Life?*

"So I lost my head over her." The mouth in Xander's head spoke easily, despite the lack of vocal cords. "Whaddaya want from me? I'm a guy. Stuff like this happens to us all the time."

"Not literally."

"Oh," Xander said. "Does this mean I went too far?"

I'm beginning to have a bad feeling about this, Buffy thought. *A really bad one.*

Could Nemesis strip her victories from her, one by one? Leave her with nothing but her fears?

What else was I afraid of screwing up? she wondered.

Come to think of it, what *hadn't* she been afraid she'd screw up?

"Hey," a new voice said.

It was Oz.

I had to ask, didn't I? Buffy thought as he half-walked, half-crawled into the light.

Though, in a strange way, Oz's appearance did make sense. He really didn't need Buffy to screw things up for him. He had plenty of problems all on his own.

"Watch out," Oz said. Something wet landed on the top of Buffy's head. Quickly, careful to avoid stepping on Xander, she dodged to one side. She raised the torch up. Slowly, an object came into view.

Something, someone, was descending from the ceiling. Buffy heard the clank of chains as the body traveled down. She put her hand to her head, then brought it into the torchlight, even though she already knew what she would find.

Just as she knew who it was that was heading straight toward her.

Blood. Willow. In that order.

This isn't real. It can't be happening, she thought.

Willow had been chained like this at the beginning of her junior year, when the followers of the Master had taken her, to use her blood in an attempt to bring him back to life.

But it didn't happen! Buffy thought again. *I stopped this, too.*

Willow shouldn't be hanging upside down with her throat cut.

"I'm sorry," Willow said. Her voice gurgled strangely. "I guess I didn't help you very much this time."

"But you did, Will. We beat him, don't you remember?"

"Sorry," Willow said again. "I'm so sorry."

"Stop it!" Buffy shouted. If anyone should be sorry, she was the one.

Willow never should have been placed in the kind of danger that could kill her in the first place. None of Buffy's friends should have.

Instead, they'd literally had their lives threatened, time and again.

And I'm the cause.

Because of who she was.

Buffy Summers. Renegade Slayer.

The one who didn't want to play by the rules, or at least not anyone's except her own. The one who never missed a chance to ignore them, break them, or best of all, to blast them straight to kingdom come. The one who put everyone and everything she loved at risk just so she could do things her way.

How many times would Buffy be able to save her friends before these nightmare images began to come true? Before her friends began to die horrible, unnatural deaths, one by one?

She could already think of one person she hadn't been able to save.

"I loved her," Giles's voice said. "I never really got the chance to tell her."

Oh, God, Buffy thought. *Please, not this.*

Giles walked toward her, cradling a dead Jenny Calendar in his arms. Buffy stood within a circle of her friends. Or what was left of them.

I'm surrounded now.

Surrounded by her past. By memories she carried with her. Feelings she'd never really lost.

Learning of Jenny's death was one of the most horrible moments Buffy'd ever faced. Because she'd known she was part of the cause. If she hadn't loved Angel, in all the ways she could—

Angel . . .

"You know there's only one way this can end, don't you?"

Angel stepped forward into the light of Buffy's torch. His dark eyes bored into hers. But then they sort of always did that. Intense eye contact being part of what made Angel what he was.

"You're the Slayer," Angel continued. "I'm a vampire. End of story. Simple plot."

"I should have thought you of all people would have figured out by now that there is nothing simple about love," Nemesis had said.

"No," Buffy said. "It's not like that. I won't let it be like that."

Angel gave her a bitter smile. "I don't think you have a choice. There's only one way this can end, and you know it. You stabbed me before. You can do it again. Only this time—" He morphed into vamp mode.

"I suggest you make it stick."

With a snarl, he lunged for her.

Buffy ducked, scooping up Xander's head and tossing it to Oz.

"Here! Catch!" she said.

"Hey," Xander protested. "Be gentle with me. I'm all I've got!"

Buffy turned to face Angel. The two began to circle.

"What's the matter?" Angel taunted. "You're the big, bad Slayer, aren't you? Why not close in? Finish me off?"

"This isn't going to work, Angel," Buffy said. "I'm not afraid of you. And you can't make me do something I don't want."

"Wanna bet?"

Without warning, Angel lunged. Buffy sidestepped. The arm that wasn't holding the torch flashed out. Buffy's first caught Angel square in the jaw, sent him staggering back.

"I'll say this for you," he said. "You do know how to pack a punch."

"You better believe it. Now back off."

"Not a chance. It's time you faced a few facts."

"Such as?"

"What you *are* afraid of."

Buffy felt a cold, sick feeling take hold in the pit of her stomach.

"You're afraid you'll lose, aren't you?" Angel taunted. "You know you are. Because you know you will. Sooner or later, you're going to come up against something even you can't beat. Something that's stronger. Then you'll be like every other Slayer in history. Dead."

"Been there. Done that," Buffy said.

"I hear it's easier the second time around," Angel answered.

Buffy felt the coldness in her stomach twist until it hurt. "Stop it," she cried. "Just stop it."

"Make me—"

Buffy hurled her torch to the ground and launched herself forward.

She kicked up, catching Angel under the chin. He staggered backward, then regained his balance.

"You're going to have to do better than that," he said.

"Don't worry," Buffy answered. "I can pretty much guarantee the hits will keep on coming."

She moved into a series of roundhouses, buffeting Angel in the chest. Then followed with a right hook. Angel blocked her. Swiftly, she brought her left arm up. He blocked that, too.

"Checkmate," he said.

Buffy brought her head forward in a connection of craniums that made her see stars and sent Angel to his knees.

"I don't think so."

She lashed out with the toe of her boot, catching Angel in the face and sending him sprawling over onto his back. Blood roaring in her ears, she jumped up and came down, hard, pinning his arms with her knees.

She reached into her jacket pocket. Whipped out a stake.

"You were saying?"

"You can't do it, can you?" Angel said. "You're too afraid."

Buffy felt fireworks explode inside her brain.

She was the Slayer. Fear was for other people. She couldn't afford to be afraid of anything.

"Chicken," she heard Angel say. "You're going to lose. You know that, don't you?"

With a cry, Buffy raised the stake above her head.

CHAPTER 13

Willow gave a high-pitched scream, twisting her head from side to side. The pain behind her eyes jabbed like a dagger.

I don't want to see this, she thought. Didn't want to watch Buffy drive a stake through Angel. Not even when she knew the real one stood right by her side.

"All right," she heard Giles's voice say. "I've seen enough."

Willow felt the bowl being lifted from her knees. A moment later, she heard the hiss of water and fire being joined. Smoke poured out into the room, making her eyes sting. Choking her.

The pain behind her eyes became a hot, white light that winked out abruptly. Willow cried out, and slumped over sideways. The only thing that prevented her head from connecting with the stone floor was Oz's arms around her.

But even through her pain, she knew what Giles had done.

Fire consumes water.

The scrying spell was over.

"I'll open a window," Angel said. A moment later, Willow felt cool air move through the room, clearing out the smoke.

"Willow," she heard Giles's voice say. "Can you hear me? How are you?"

"Okay, I think," she said. She sat up slowly. Her head still pounded, but the pain wasn't so bad now.

"How many fingers am I holding up?" Xander cut in, waving his hand in front of her face.

"Will you please *stop* that?" Giles snapped.

"Just trying to help," Xander mumbled.

"You're certain you're all right?" Giles asked, peering at Willow intently. "How's the head?"

Willow gave him a wavering smile. "Having an extra-strength Tylenol kind of moment."

Giles leaned back. "Not altogether surprising. That spell was far too dangerous for you, Willow. I do *not* recommend you try that again."

"You didn't recommend she try it this time," Angel said, as he came back into the room.

"Hey," Willow protested. "I thought you were on *my* side."

"I think we're all on the same side here," Oz said.

"Well, yeah," Willow said, "but, what do we do now? We're right back to where we started. We don't know what's happening. We're in the dark."

"And we may just have to stay there," said Giles.

"The terms of Buffy's trial specifically stipulated that she go alone."

"Wait a minute," Angel interrupted.

"Oh for—of course," Giles exclaimed. "Why didn't I think of that?"

"But we don't know where it is," Willow protested.

"Why am I beginning to get that last-one-in's-a-rotten-egg feeling?" Xander asked.

"I know," Angel said.

"What?" Giles exploded.

"I know where the trial is."

"Well, why didn't you say so before now?"

"I didn't think of it before now. Besides, you never asked."

"Where is Buffy's trial?"

"Two thousand Elysian Fields Lane."

"Right," Giles said. He got to his feet. "Let's just see what happens if we shake things up a bit around here, shall we?"

"Will somebody please tell me what's going on?" Xander nearly whined.

"Nemesis said Buffy had to go alone, but she didn't say she had to *stay* alone," Willow told him.

"Does that mean we're doing what I think we're doing?"

Willow nodded. "Scooby Gang to the rescue."

"Excellent."

The stake whistled through the air as Buffy brought it down, straight toward Angel's unprotected chest. At the last second, she pulled up.

"All right. You can cancel the subscription to *Psychology Today*. I get it," she shouted.

Took me long enough.

She stood up, releasing Angel and throwing the stake away with one violent motion. She walked to her guttering torch without looking back.

It wasn't going to last much longer, she thought. And she still hadn't found her mom, let alone the way to get her out.

Maybe Angel was right. Maybe she was going to lose.

Don't think that way, she told herself. That's playing into Nemesis's hands. Playing her game.

"What's down there? Monsters?"

"Got it in one," the Balancer had said.

But Buffy was finally beginning to realize that it was what else Nemesis had said that was most important.

"Though what kind is entirely up to you."

At the time, Buffy'd figured Nemesis was just being Ms. Cryptic Supernatural Being. Now, she knew that she hadn't.

Nemesis hadn't been cryptic. She'd been telling the truth.

And if that wasn't sneaky and underhanded, Buffy didn't know what was.

Not only did she have to undergo some stupid trial. She had to bring her own monsters.

That's what I've been doing, she realized suddenly. Battling her own fears. The ones she pushed to the back of her mind during the day. That crept back out to haunt her dreams at night. The ones that showed her friends mutilated, killed, or worse.

And always, she was at fault. She was to blame.

"You know there's only one way this can end, don't you?" Angel's voice asked again.

"Yes, I know it."

As if her words had been some sort of signal, her friends vanished. A thing she'd pretty much been expecting.

What's down here? Monsters, she thought.

Absolutely.

And the biggest one of all was—

"Hi, I'm Buffy. What's your name?" a voice directly in front of her said.

The one named Buffy Summers.

Suz Tompkins woke up slowly. Which she supposed was better than waking up dead.

Her throat felt like someone had jabbed it with an ice pick, then dragged sandpaper around inside it. She could see the blood staining the front of her jacket when she looked down. She couldn't feel her arms or her legs.

Was that the ropes, or loss of blood? she wondered.

Not that it really mattered, either way.

What mattered was that she'd been staked out like a lamb to the slaughter. She was bait.

And purely for effect, Mama Walker had bitten her. Just a little.

Suz could feel something rise up, hot and sharp inside her chest.

Rage, pure and unadulterated.

Nobody treats me this way.

Somehow, she would get herself out of this. Somehow, she would find the way. And when she did, the thing that had done this to her had better watch out.

Nobody messed with Suz Tompkins and got away with it.

Not even something that was dead already.

Buffy Summers stared.

In the light of her torch, she could just see her own image, looking for all the world as if she'd just stepped out of the pages of the scrapbook her mother was creating. A young girl of about eight, dressed in a Power Girl costume.

The younger Buffy's face was tilted up, her eyes bright as she studied her older counterpart.

Does she know it's me—it's us? Buffy thought. Did this young self know that, in spite of all the odds, she'd actually grow up to be something resembling a superhero?

Buffy was just about to answer the question when a second voice chimed in.

"Hi, I'm Buffy. What's your name?"

Oh, God, she thought. *I'm everywhere.*

From out of the shadows they came, first one Buffy, then another, until the Slayer was surrounded by them. Two Buffys. Four Buffys. Six. Eight. Ten. Twelve. Until there were more versions of herself than she could count.

And she remembered every one of them.

There she was in the fancy dress she'd worn for sixth-grade graduation. Standing beside her was a somewhat younger version, dressed for ice skating. That little blond girl was wearing what Buffy remembered as her favorite skating outfit. A white shirt with a Peter Pan collar. A red flannel circle skirt that had rippled around her when she whirled through her turns.

She saw herself as a cheerleader, right before being called as the Slayer. As a young girl dressed in pajamas with feet, a gap in her smile as she grinned and held up one palm to proudly display her very first lost tooth. As far as she could see, there were Buffys.

They're me, she thought. *I'm them.*

What was so bad about that?

"Hi, I'm Buffy. What's your name?" Power Girl Buffy asked once more. And the Slayer felt the final piece of the puzzle slide into place in her brain.

It was Willow who'd given her the key.

Nemesis: an agent or act of retribution.

Okay, Buffy thought. *Got that.* She was here at the trial, wasn't she? Vamp Mama's revenge.

Someone or something that defeats or destroys one.

Her own fears, for instance. Like the ones where she couldn't save her friends from getting dead.

An opponent whom one cannot best.

Gee, now who would that be? she wondered.

Buffy'd had to fight lots of things in her career as the Slayer, including a couple of things that had come close to doing her in. Way too close for comfort.

But there was only one opponent she knew beyond a shadow of a doubt would match her every action, every thought. Just one opponent who, no matter how hard she tried, Buffy would never be able to best.

I knew I was going to have to kick some butts when I came here, Buffy thought. She just hadn't figured so many of them would turn out to be her own.

"Hi, I'm Buffy Summers," Buffy said. "I'm the Slayer. And you're not. You're in my way. I think you should get out of it. Right now."

The Buffy closest to her, one wearing a Halloween cat costume, laughed and pressed a little closer.

"Okay, have it your way," Buffy said. She never had known when to quit.

The Slayer reached out, and gave her younger self a sharp shove. With a yelp, the other Buffy tumbled backward, knocking into the Buffy behind her, starting a chain reaction. Buffys began toppling over like dominoes. Shattering like mirrors as they hit the basement's hard concrete floor. Forming tiny little Buffy shards.

Those Buffys that were still standing began to panic, flinging themselves upon the Slayer, biting, scratching, trying to pull her down.

Buffy lost track of how many selves she battled. The torch was knocked from her hand. And still they came, and the ground at Buffy's feet grew thick with their pieces as she shattered and vanquished them. These images of the girl she had been but could never be again.

And then they were gone. All but one.

Buffy found herself staring into the eyes of the first image she'd encountered. The one in the Power Girl costume. Across the sea of broken Buffys, the two girls looked at one another. Then the young Buffy lifted her chin, a gesture the Slayer recognized as a direct challenge. A tiny smile flitted across the younger Buffy's mouth. Without a word, she turned and fled.

Stopping only to scoop her almost dead torch from the floor, the Slayer followed.

CHAPTER 14

I really hope she knows where she's going.

Through the darkened basement, the Slayer pursued her younger self. Till her breath began to come in ragged gasps and the torch went out.

Buffy hardly noticed. Because now, she could see something up ahead, something that glowed through the darkness. Not a nice, comforting glow, like the lighted windows of your own house on a cold winter's night, but a sickly green glare that in Buffy's experience always meant just one thing.

She had reached her final destination. The lair of the last monster.

What would it be this time? she wondered. Demons? More vampires? Some Underworld buddies of Nemesis's, along for the ride?

As Buffy watched, her younger self slowed to a walk, then stopped and turned, her eyes expectant as they looked at Buffy. As if she were waiting for her, wanting them to make the final few steps of the journey together, the Slayer thought.

Either that or she was simply afraid to go on alone. Understandable. And very likely. Buffy wasn't all that wild about finding out herself. But that wasn't going to stop her from doing whatever it took to save her mother.

She threw down her useless torch. She didn't need it anymore anyway. The glare was strong now, though she still couldn't see what caused it. The basement turned just up ahead. Whatever was causing that sick green glow was just around the corner.

Plainly, Nemesis was into a little suspense.

Well, there's no time like the present, Buffy thought. She stepped up beside her younger self and reached down to take Power Girl Buffy's hand. Her younger self's fingers were hot as they closed around hers, but their grip was determined.

Together, the two Buffys stepped around the corner, then stopped short.

Give me a break, Buffy thought.

She supposed she should have known. It wasn't her biggest fear, not by a long shot. But it went all the way back to her childhood, where it ranked right up there with fear of the dark.

Not death. Not demons. Not vampires. Those fears had come much later. The thing that had stalked the nightmares of her childhood was . . .

Spiders.

Or, actually, in this case, simply *spider.*

As in the biggest spider Buffy'd ever seen, and her

nightmares back then had conjured up some whoppers.

This one looked half as tall as she was at least, and a whole lot wider. Its segmented body was the soft white color Buffy always associated with cottage cheese. Its bulbous abdomen was covered with angry red splotches.

It looked like some enormous bloodshot eye. Either that, or a really bad case of chicken pox.

A case of chicken pox that glowed in the dark.

A thing Buffy figured she could use to her advantage. It was pretty hard for things that glowed in the dark to sneak up on you.

In the lower right corner of the web was what looked like a big, white lozenge.

Egg sac, Buffy thought. How come she always ended up fighting something that was about to be a mother? The Bezoar, Natalie French, and now this. Maybe she needed Slayer family counseling or something.

"Your name wouldn't happen to be Charlotte, would it?"

At the sound of Buffy's voice, the spider scuttled forward. It lifted its forelegs, as if in answer to a challenge. Now Buffy could see what was behind the spider, in the topmost corner of the web, hidden by its great, splotchy body.

It was Joyce.

"Mom!" Buffy cried out. Beside her, she heard her younger self make a sound of dismay. Joyce's head turned toward them. Buffy saw her mother wince as her action caused the spider thread to pull against her hair.

"Buffy," Joyce said. Her voice sounded thin and weak. Buffy felt a finger of pure ice slide down her spine. Another few minutes and she might have been too late.

"Honey, if that's you . . . don't come any closer."

I don't think so, Mom. Buffy hadn't come all this way just to stand around and chat. She released her hold on her younger self's hand and moved forward.

Instantly, the spider moved, too, dancing backward, closer to Joyce. There was no way Buffy could get to her mom before the spider did.

Buffy stopped. The spider stopped.

Checkmate. Impasse.

The Slayer considered her options.

A little distraction might come in handy right about now. Too bad her chances of creating one didn't look very likely. She couldn't distract the spider and save her mom at the same time.

Not even the Slayer can be in two places at once.

Buffy felt a tug on her arm. Her younger self had moved to stand beside her once more. The younger Buffy looked up at the Slayer, as if she, too, was considering her options. Then she moved toward the web. Straight toward the corner that held the egg sac.

Buffy felt a tingle dance along the surface of her skin. Watching her younger self was like experiencing déjà vu for a situation Buffy knew had never happened. She didn't have to wonder what the girl in the Power Girl costume walking so steadily toward the giant spider web was going to do next. She already knew.

She was going to provide the Slayer with her distraction.

Without warning, a surge of fierce, unbridled joy shot through Buffy. She could almost feel a light bulb go off above her head. The coin drop. The background music swell as the chorus came in.

About time, she thought.

She got it.

Got why her mom had wanted to put a scrapbook together in the first place. Got the thing this younger version of herself was trying to show her.

She was that girl; she was all those other Buffys. The fact that she'd grown up to be something none of them could have predicted didn't mean that she'd betrayed them, that she had to leave them all behind. She hadn't grown up to be nothing more than a freak, a disappointment.

She wasn't her own nemesis. She didn't have to fight herself. Be the opponent she could never hope to best. Instead, she could be part of a never-ending chain of Buffys. Every single one of them a part of what had brought her to this moment.

If she won now, they all passed the test.

And all she had to do was to genuinely embrace the things she was now. All the things that she had been. She didn't have to beat her other selves to save her mother. What she had to do was join them.

Buffy looked at her younger self. The girl was staring at the egg sac. Buffy reached into the pocket of her jacket, felt her hand close around the one stake she had left. She pulled it out and tossed it to the girl who caught it easily.

For a moment, her younger self stared up at the Slayer. Then she switched her attention to the sharp, jagged end of the stake. She cocked her head to one side.

"Go for it," the Slayer said.

The younger Buffy's grin flashed out. She grasped

the stake firmly by the thicker end, and jabbed the sharp end straight into the very center of the egg sac.

The mother spider reacted at once. Rushing across the web, hissing as she pelted toward them. Halfway between Joyce and the two Buffys, the giant spider stopped. Her forelegs beat the air in agitation. Buffy could have sworn she read her mind.

Always assuming spiders had minds, of course.

Defending her captive or her children, which was more important? The spider inched closer.

Children.

Buffy smiled over at her younger self. "Nice going," she commented.

Her younger self looked up once more, her eyes shining. She held the stake out toward Buffy.

"Okay, I'll take it from here," the Slayer said. She reached out to grab the stake. For one last time, Buffy felt the touch of her younger self's fingers. Then, the contact was gone. Her younger self vanished. Buffy was left standing alone by the egg sac, holding the stake in her hand.

Now that I've got myself together, she thought.

It was time for action.

"Get away from my mother."

Gripping the stake tightly in her fist, Buffy raised it above the egg sac, then brought it down.

The mother spider abandoned Joyce and rushed to save her children as a gelatinous mass burst from the sac and began to spread across the floor. Ignoring the various blobs, Buffy skirted the bottom of the web, put the stake in her mouth like a pirate dagger, and began to climb up to reach her mom.

The spider silk clung to her hands and feet, making her progress agonizingly slow. *Hurry,* she thought. *Hurry.*

At any moment, she expected to feel the spider at her back. Buffy really hated to leave her back exposed, but it was the only way she could get to Joyce. Only one more part of the trial to go now.

Buffy had discovered the trial's secret. She was about to get her mother. That just left the part where they got out. Alive.

She reached her mother, began to hack away at the strands that held her.

"It's all right. I'm here, Mom. Can you walk?"

She saw Joyce swallow. She opened her mouth to speak, but no sound came out.

"Mom, I really need you to answer me," Buffy said. "Do you think that you can walk when we get down?"

Joyce nodded weakly. Managed to speak the second time around. "I think so," she said. "But I . . . don't feel very well. Full of spider venom, probably."

Don't think about it, Buffy told herself fiercely as she freed Joyce's arms.

Spider venom. Her mother. How it got there. Not a combination Buffy cared to dwell on.

"Maybe you should go first," Joyce said, as Buffy sawed through the bindings on her legs. "Let me catch up."

"Forget about it, Mom," Buffy said as Joyce's knees buckled and she tumbled forward. Buffy scrambled down the web, the sticky strands pulling the skin from her hands, and caught her mother a split second before she hit the cement floor. She pulled her upright, then helped her peel away the web.

"Maybe moving will help," she suggested. "You know, get the old circulation going."

"Maybe," Joyce muttered. "Only . . . Buffy . . ."

"What?" the Slayer said, trying not to sound testy. Didn't her mom get that this was a rescue op? "Mom, this really isn't the greatest time for a heart-to-heart talk, you know."

"I know," Joyce said. "It's just—whatever the plan is, we should probably get right on it, honey."

Buffy spun around, instinctively making sure her mother's body was blocked by her own.

The spider was right behind her.

Buffy could see the series of beady red eyes on the spider's head. Swear she could feel putrid spider breath flowing toward her. The spider took one mincing step.

"Uh uh," Buffy said, raising the stake. "I don't think so."

Lunging forward, she made a great diagonal sweep with her arm, slashing across the spider's face. Several of the red eyes winked out. The spider fell back, beating its hairy forelegs in the air.

"Come on," Buffy said, grabbing Joyce by the arm. "We're going."

She took two steps, making sure her mom went first, and then the spider was upon her, slashing at Buffy's back and arms.

"Mom, go!" Buffy commanded as she turned and lashed out with the stake. Green goo oozed where she connected with a spider foreleg. Buffy leaped back. The last thing she needed was to be covered in spider slime. *Think of the dry cleaning.*

She connected sharply with her mother and stumbled.

"Why are you still here?" Buffy said as she regained her balance. The spider scuttled forward once more, favoring its right foreleg. Buffy crouched, passing the stake from hand to hand.

"I can't just leave you," Joyce answered from behind her.

"Mom, you really need to trust me on this one. This is no time for parental heroics. The only way we're both going to get out of here is if you go first."

Buffy watched the spider pull its legs in. *Uh oh.* She had a *very* bad feeling she knew what was going to come next.

"But—"

"Just go!" Buffy said. Behind her, she heard her mother take a few faltering steps.

The spider jumped, landing precisely where Joyce had been just an instant before. Now, it was between Buffy and her mother. Good old divide and conquer. From the far side of the monstrosity, Buffy heard Joyce cry out.

She took several steps back, then launched herself forward in a great running leap.

She pivoted in midair, reaching up and to the right, aiming for the underside of the joint on the closest of the spider's big back legs. Green slime gushed out around her as the stake bit deep.

Buffy landed, her feet shooting out from under her as she hit ground in a pool of spider slime. She went down, hard, flat on her back on the floor of the basement, the air punching from her lungs.

How come I never get to fall on anything soft? she

wondered as she watched the spots dance before her eyes, then saw her vision dim.

Why did it always have to be hard? Cement. Pavement. Stone floors of crypts. That sort of thing.

Would it break some major Slayer rule if I got to land on something a little less potentially bone-breaking for a change? Something that didn't help her adversary just by being what it was?

One more thing to ask Giles, she thought. Assuming she ever made it out of here and so got to ask him anything. She shook her head, trying to clear her vision.

But the dim, shifting mass in front of her didn't disappear. She was under the spider. *I really should try to get up.* Because if she didn't, she had a feeling the spider was going to do something totally disgusting.

Such as squashing her like a bug.

It was backing up, waggling its abdomen as if jockeying into position. No time to roll out of the way. Buffy barely had time to pull her knees up and roll over onto her side before the spider abdomen began to descend.

I am not doing a Little Miss Muffet.

Buffy pushed herself to her knees, then extended the arm holding the stake. She heard the spider shriek once more as the point connected. But in spite of its soft appearance, the skin on the spider abdomen was tough and thick.

Still, the abdomen descended.

It folded on either side of Buffy until the Slayer began to fear that she'd be suffocated.

Who knew you could play chicken with arachnids?

If Buffy pulled back now, she'd be squashed for sure. If the spider didn't pull up, it ran the risk of being skewered.

Whose will was stronger? The Slayer's or the spider's? And—did spiders actually have free will?

Okay, Buffy thought. *Enough's enough*. If she was so far gone she was beginning to contemplate philosophical questions in the middle of a fight, it was definitely time to get things rolling. She couldn't crouch here all night. She had a mother to think of.

She put her free hand down, using it to leverage herself up into a crouch. She could feel the arm holding the stake start to quiver as the pressure from the spider became greater. Buffy locked her elbow.

I get to count on my own this time, Angel, she thought. One. Two. As usual, she never really got to three.

The Slayer pushed up abruptly. She could feel the spider skin above her give as the point of the stake finally penetrated. With an ear-splitting shriek, the spider pulled up. Not much. But it was enough.

Buffy released her hold on the stake and made a twisting leap into the air, rolling and kicking out with her right leg, jamming it into the part of the stake that was still exposed. She felt the give as it punched all the way through. The spider howled in pain, its body jerking upward. A great gush of slime cascaded over Buffy.

There's always slime.

This time, she didn't even try to keep her balance. She landed on her stomach on the floor of the basement and pushed herself forward with her arms, hydroplaning out from beneath the spider's body.

The wounded spider was going wild, scuttling back and forth, careening wildly. Its abdomen gyrated as it tried to shake the stake loose. Buffy heard a sickening *splat* as it connected with a wall. Bits of plaster from the ceiling rained down upon her head. The walls of the basement began to tremble around her.

We've got to get out of here now, she thought. *Before the spider brings the whole house down on us.*

"Mom!" she cried out.

Silence. Or as silent as things could be when sharing a space with a giant spider in the midst of death throes.

Buffy's heart began to pound in her throat. Where was her mother?

The spider was on its back now, beating its legs in the air. Buffy cut a wide circle around it. A few steps beyond, she found her mother crumpled on the floor.

For one heart-stopping moment Buffy feared her mother was dead. That she hadn't been fast enough. Then she realized she could see her mother's chest rise and fall in shallow breaths, and that her eyes were open, staring up at her.

"Mom, we really have to go *now.*"

"I know that, sweetheart," her mother said. "It's just—I think I need your help."

"We'll go together, Mom," the Slayer said.

She helped Joyce to her feet, then hurried her through the basement. The way grew lighter the farther they went, as if to acknowledge that Buffy was no longer in the dark. She had passed her tests. She could see her way now.

No shards of Buffys. No Xander's head.

Now, there was only one thing left.

Buffy and Joyce reached the bottom of the basement stairs. The first monster's ashes were gone, the bottom stair replaced. "Come on," Buffy urged. "Just a little bit farther."

Just these stairs, and then they'd be free. Buffy went first, pulling her mother up behind her.

She reached the door. Tried the knob.

It was locked.

"Oh, give me a major break." Buffy lifted one foot and kicked. The door crashed back upon its hinges. Then Buffy was through the opening, pulling her mother after her. She kicked the door closed, then let Joyce lean back against it as she once more slumped to Buffy's feet. Her knees suddenly weak, Buffy eased down beside her.

It was all right to relax now. She had done it. They were out of the basement. The trial was over. Her mom was safe.

I did it. I won.

She turned her head to look at Joyce and found her mother's eyes already upon her.

"I really hope that's not some new skin-care product you have your heart set on using," Joyce said weakly, wiping some slime from Buffy's face. "Because I have to tell you, it smells just awful."

"Bubble bath, as soon as I get home," Buffy promised. She took her mother's hand in hers, squeezed hard. "We did it, Mom. We won. We can go home."

"*You* did it, you mean," answered her mother. She squeezed back. "I suppose that means you want me to get up now."

"Unless you'd like to stay here for a while."

"Not likely," Joyce said.

Slowly, the two got to their feet.

"I feel like I have a bad hangover," Joyce said.

"As opposed to a good one?" Buffy asked. She

linked her arm with her mother's. Together they crossed the kitchen, heading for the living room.

Joyce turned her head from side to side, her expression bemused as she took in the floral wallpaper

"Who on earth lives here?" she asked.

"No one you want to know," Buffy said, wondering where Nemesis was, when was the trial officially over?

She glanced down at their feet, helping to guide her mom's still shaky footsteps down the short flight of steps that led to the sunken living room.

"It's just through here, then across the—"

"Buffy," her mother said. It was not the tone of voice that went with her happy face.

Buffy's head shot up. She stopped dead in her tracks.

On the far side of the living room, a figure was stretched on one of the uncomfortable sofas. Its feet were tied over the arms of the sofa to one set of wooden legs, its hands to the other.

As Buffy watched, the figure slowly raised its head. Its features were pale and waxy. Even from across the room, Buffy could see the slight trail of blood that ran down one side of its neck.

"*Suz?*"

"Buffy—" Suz rasped. "I thought—"

"She thought she had it all figured out," a voice behind Buffy said.

She pivoted swiftly, pulling her mother around behind her.

"The same way you do," Zahalia Walker said. "But I wouldn't be too sure about anything, if I were you. You're not leaving here until I finish with you first."

CHAPTER 15

"**W**ait a minute!" Xander said. "I think you were supposed to turn right."

"Stop back-seat driving," Giles snapped. He executed as smart a U-turn as his car would allow, passing Oz's van, which was following along behind him. A squeal of brakes indicated Oz had turned too.

"I'm not sitting in back," Xander countered. "I'm sitting in front, next to you. In America, we call this the passenger side."

"Will you stop nattering on and let me concentrate?" Giles inquired. "I don't know this part of town very well."

"A point even I can see is obvious—Hey!" Xander yelled as the Citroën's own tires squealed around a corner. "You were supposed to take a left there, Giles!"

"I distinctly recall you telling me it was a right turn."

"That was when we were going in the opposite direction."

"Oh, bloody hell."

Buffy put her hands on her hips and faced the vampire mother.

"What is your problem?" she demanded. "Don't you know when to quit? You asked for the trial. You got one. You lost. I won. I get to take my mother out of here. Fade to black. End of story. And nobody said you got to snack on my friends."

"There have been some revisions," said Zahalia Walker. "Nobody kills my boys and walks away, including you, Slayer. Nemesis or no Nemesis. You passed the trial, but you won't get past me."

"We'll just see about that," Buffy said. "Mom. Go. Now."

"I'm not—" Joyce Summers started.

"Just do it!" the Slayer shouted. Then she lowered her head and ran straight at Zahalia Walker.

The mother vampire gave a grunt as Buffy's head rammed into her stomach. She fell back, her hands scrabbling for purchase on Buffy's shoulders. The Slayer let the vampire's momentum pull them both down, then kept on rolling. She somersaulted over Vamp Mama's head, then vaulted to her feet and spun around. Zahalia Walker was still getting to her feet.

The trial's over. Mama Vamp is fair game. So where's a good stake when I really need one?

"I'm going to kill you," Mrs. Walker taunted as she got to her feet. "I'm going to kill you and I'm going to make your mother watch. Just like I had to watch you kill my Webster. Then I'm going to make your mother one of us. It's so hard to find a good bridge partner in this day and age."

"You're not getting anywhere near her," Buffy said.

"Try and stop me."

Almost before the vampire mother had finished speaking, Buffy was in motion. She leaped forward with a roundhouse kick that sent the vampire crashing sideways. She followed it up with a kick to the chest. The vampire mother smacked up against the wall. One of her fat fists shot out, catching Buffy full in the face. The Slayer staggered back.

Ow.

"If I need a nose job, you're paying for it."

Zahalia Walker laughed. "By the time I'm finished with you, Slayer, you won't care about your nose. You won't have a face anymore."

Buffy caught a quick glimpse of motion from the corner of her eye. Her mother had Suz's arms untied and was working on her legs.

Way to go, Mom.

The vampire mother began to ease toward Joyce and Suz. Buffy shifted to block her. She had to keep herself between them at all costs.

That thing's not getting my mother.

"Why don't you just attack me, Slayer?" Zahalia Walker asked. "Could it be that you're getting tired? I can keep on going all night. I've got forever. But not you. You're mortal."

"Not to mention bored to tears," Buffy said.

Why do I always get the chatty vampires?

But much as she hated to admit it, Vamp Mama was

right. Buffy *was* mortal. And she *was* tired. Her arms felt heavy. Her legs, wobbly.

"And just what *is* that disgusting substance you're tracking all over my beautiful carpet?" continued the vampire mother. "What were you, raised in a barn or something? I'm going to have to have a talk with your mother. Before I drink her blood, of course."

Buffy cast another quick glance over her shoulder at her mother. Suz's legs were free now, too. Joyce was rubbing them, trying to get the circulation going. Slowly, Buffy began to edge to one side of the living room, aiming for a small table that stood against the wall.

Suz and Joyce were on their feet now, moving toward the hall.

"You don't actually think I'm going to let them get away, do you?" asked the vampire mother.

Now or never, Buffy thought.

She leaped for the table just as the vampire mother hurled herself toward her. She hit Buffy full on. Together, the two crashed down against the table, sending pieces flying. Buffy smacked against the wall, then slid down. She could feel sharp pieces of wood jabbing into her back as she landed on the floor, the wind knocked out of her.

Don't stake yourself, you idiot! The vampire! The vampire!

Buffy had lots of wood now. The trouble would be getting them into action. First, she had to get her breath back. And then she had to get the vampire off of her.

Zahalia Walker had her hands in Buffy's hair. She lifted the Slayer's head, then slammed it back against the floor. Once. Twice.

"Those are for Webster and Percy," said the vampire

mother. She slammed Buffy's head down a third time, then jerked it to one side. The Slayer could feel her pulse beating like a wild thing. She tried to buck, but Zahalia Walker's immense frame had her pinned down.

"And this," she said, bringing her face close as her jaws opened. "This one is for me."

"I beg your pardon." Through eyes that still saw stars, Buffy saw a hand tap the vampire mother on the shoulder. "Excuse me," the familiar voice went on. "I'm so sorry to be a bother."

With a snarl, Zahalia Walker turned around. Apparently, even her instinct to kill was no match for all those years of proper etiquette.

"What?" she snarled.

"This," said Joyce Summers.

A moment later, Buffy found herself lying in a pile of vampire dust. Suz Tompkins stood above her, a table leg clenched in one fist, the jagged end pointing down at Buffy.

"That was for Leila and Heidi."

"Well done," said the voice of the Balancer.

"About time you showed up," Buffy said. "You aren't by any chance familiar with the concept of fair play, are you?"

She pushed herself into a sitting position, then let Suz pull her to her feet. Buffy felt totally disgusting. The vampire dust was adhering to the spider goo.

She heard a crash from the front hall. *Now what?*

"This better not be anyone you know," she told the Balancer.

She watched in astonishment as Angel sprang into the room, Giles and Willow right behind him. Oz was backing Willow up. And Xander was backing up . . . everybody.

Giles skidded to a halt at the sight of Nemesis.

"Ah," she said, her faces grinning. "This must be the faithful Watcher."

"The Balancer, I presume?" Giles remarked calmly.

Buffy heard her mother give a snort of laughter.

I did it, Buffy thought. *This time, I really have won.*

"I think the cavalry just arrived," Joyce said.

Buffy grinned at her friends. "Hey, guys. Great timing."

CHAPTER 16

"**B**ut I still don't get why that Nemesis-Balancer-deity-thing didn't interfere when the vampire mother attacked Buffy," said Xander. "I mean, that does seem like a pretty clear foul ball."

It was an hour or so later and all the parties involved in the evening's events were sitting in the Summers's kitchen, polishing off enormous bowls of ice cream. Or, all of them except for Angel and Buffy's mother.

Joyce had pleaded extreme weariness and had gone to bed. And it was just a little too close to sunrise for Angel to feel comfortable hanging out in Buffy's kitchen consuming cold dairy products.

And then there was the fact that vampires didn't eat ice cream.

"Actually," Giles said, as he spooned up the last of

his Neopolitan. "I thought Nemesis herself provided a remarkably succinct explanation."

"Which probably explains why I'm still in the dark," Xander nodded.

"He's trying to say it was all my fault," said Suz Tompkins. At Buffy's insistence, Suz had accompanied the group to Buffy's home. She'd needed some first aid, for one thing. Joyce and Giles had supplied it. Plus Buffy had to figure the other girl had a few questions on her mind.

"On the contrary," Giles countered. "The vampire mother was totally obsessed by her sons. My guess would be she never intended to let Buffy leave unscathed, once she won the trial."

"The scathing thing," Willow shuddered. "I hate that part."

Buffy watched as Suz's head swiveled back and forth between Willow and Giles.

"I still can't believe you actually did a scrying spell, Will," she said. "That's pretty major stuff."

"It was," Willow nodded gingerly. "I know. But I feel okay now. Still four-oh."

"About Nemesis," Xander prompted.

"Right," said Giles. "Well. Letting—" He glanced at Suz, as if uncertain what to call her. "Letting Ms. Tompkins dispatch the vampire mother does have a certain symmetry, you know. After all, it was her sons who . . ." his voice trailed off.

"Killed my friends," Suz filled in for him.

"Yes," said Giles. He set his spoon in his empty bowl. "Well. Allowing you to kill the mother completed the circle. The overall conflict, not just between Buffy and Mrs. Walker. Restored balance. Order. I imagine Nemesis was quite satisfied by the larger outcome."

"Either that or the whole thing was rigged to begin with," Buffy said.

"Yes," Giles conceded. "It could be that, also."

He stood up and carried his bowl to the sink. He rinsed it out, then set it on the drainboard.

"What are you doing?" Buffy said.

"Dishes," Giles answered. "It's one of those skills you'll learn when you're on your own. Well, I think it's time to be off. There is actually school tomorrow."

"I don't feel so good all of a sudden," Xander said.

"Ride?" Oz asked Suz. He and Willow got up and took their bowls over to the sink.

"No, thanks," Suz said shortly. She, too, got to her feet.

"We don't like, *have* to do that dish thing, do we?" Xander inquired. " 'Cause I'm still not quite sure I've grasped the basics."

"Leave it," Buffy said. She walked her friends to the front door.

"Thanks for the ice cream," Willow said.

"Yeah," Xander seconded. "Those frosty calories always hit the spot."

Oz put his arm around Willow's shoulder. "Later."

Together, Oz, Willow and Xander headed down the front walk.

"Yes, well," Giles said. "Um, good night's work, I'd say, all in all." He followed the others, then climbed into his much-treasured Citroën.

"You're sure you don't want a ride?" Buffy asked

Suz, as the other girl lingered beside her on the porch. "I could ask Giles."

Together, they watched as Giles started his ancient car. Smoke came out the back.

Suz shook her head. "I'll get there faster if I walk."

"Giles is not exactly Mister Macho Car Man, I admit. But he's a pretty good guy."

"So—" Suz said, as they watched the others drive away. "About tonight . . ."

Here it comes, Buffy thought. "What about it?"

"That thing I killed really was a vampire, wasn't it?"

"Yes," Buffy said simply. "It really was."

"And her sons, they were the ones who killed my friends?"

Buffy nodded.

"You took them down."

"I dusted them, all right. That's kind of a special technical term we have for killing vampires."

"The vampire mother called you something—had some special name for you."

"The Slayer," Buffy replied.

"And that's what—something you do for fun?"

"No," Buffy replied. "Fun is going to the movies and eating too much buttered popcorn. Being the Slayer is what I am. It's kind of like my job."

"And Mister Giles is what—your boss?"

"Sort of more like a supervisor," Buffy answered.

"And your friends—they know what you are. They even help you."

Buffy nodded. "It's part of the whole friend concept."

Suz looked at her through tired eyes.

"So, I guess we're not so different after all," she said. "You have your friends, I have mine."

Had, Buffy thought. "Well, we definitely have a different tolerance for body piercing."

Suz smiled.

"I'm sorry about Heidi and Leila," Buffy said. *Now I know how I would feel.*

"Yeah, thanks."

"Are you going to be all right?"

"Sure. Thanks for satisfying my curiosity."

As if she'd said everything there was to say, Suz started down the steps. Halfway down the front walk she stopped.

"Buffy," she said, turning back.

"Yeah?"

"Don't lose your balance."

"I'll try not to," the Slayer said.

She was smiling as she watched the girl in the camouflage jacket disappear into the darkness.

ABOUT THE AUTHOR

Cameron Dokey (yes, her real name, and she does know everything that rhymes with it) is completely delighted to be working for the Slayer. She's been a fan ever since she watched the Chosen One put an end to Pee Wee Herman in that first feature film. Cameron is also the author of more than twenty novels for young adults, including *Love Me, Love Me Not,* singled out by the New York Public Library as a Best Book for Teens. She lives in Seattle, Washington, with three cats, one husband, and a collection of more than fifty old sci-fi and horror films.

"Wish me monsters."

—Buffy, "Living Conditions"

Vampires, werewolves, witches, demons of nonspecific origin...

They're all here in this extensive guide to the monsters of *Buffy* and their mythological, literary, and cultural origins.

Includes interviews with the show's writers and creator Joss Whedon

Buffy the Vampire Slayer™

THE MONSTER BOOK

By
Christopher Golden
(co-author of THE WATCHER'S GUIDE)
Stephen R. Bissett
Thomas E. Sniegoski

FROM

POCKET BOOKS

2809

Everyone's got his demons....

ANGEL™

**If it takes an eternity,
he will make amends.**

Original stories based on the
TV show created by Joss Whedon
& David Greenwalt

Available from Pocket Pulse
Published by Pocket Books

. . . A GIRL BORN
WITHOUT THE FEAR GENE

FEARLESS™

A NEW SERIES BY
FRANCINE PASCAL

A TITLE AVAILABLE EVERY MONTH

From Pocket Pulse
Published by Pocket Books